The
Proposal

Christy Fiction Series

Christy Fiction Series

The
Proposal

Catherine Marshall

adapted by C. Archer

WORD PUBLISHING
Dallas・London・Vancouver・Melbourne

THE PROPOSAL
Book Five in the *Christy* Fiction Series

Managing Editor: Laura Minchew
Project Editor: Beverly Phillips

Library of Congress Cataloging-in-Publication Data

Archer, C. 1956–
    The proposal / Catherine Marshall ; adapted by C. Archer.
        p.   cm. — (Christy fiction series ; 5)
    "Word kids!"
    Summary: Blinded in a riding accident, Christy has self-doubts
about resuming her career as a missionary teacher and accepting the
town minister's marriage proposal.
    ISBN 0–8499–3918–6 (pbk.)
    [1. Teachers—Fiction 2. Blind—Fiction. 3. Physically handi-
capped—Fiction. 4. Mountain life—Fiction. 5. Christian life—
Fiction.] I. Marshall, Catherine, 1914–1983. Christy. II. Title.
III. Series : Archer, C., 1956–   Christy fiction series ; 5.
    PZ7.A6744Pr   1996
    [Fic]—dc20

                                                        95–53078
                                                            CIP
                                                             AC

Printed in the United States of America

97 98 99 00 OPM 9 8 7 6 5 4 3 2

The Characters

CHRISTY RUDD HUDDLESTON, a nineteen-year-old girl.

CHRISTY'S STUDENTS:
    CREED ALLEN, age nine.
    LITTLE BURL ALLEN, age six.
    WANDA BECK, age eight.
    BESSIE COBURN, age twelve.
    LIZETTE HOLCOMBE, age fifteen.
    SAM HOUSTON HOLCOMBE, age nine.
    WRAIGHT HOLT, age seventeen.
    ZACHARIAS HOLT, age nine.
    VELLA HOLT, age five.
    SMITH O'TEALE, age fifteen.
    ORTER BALL O'TEALE, age eleven.
    MOUNTIE O'TEALE, age ten.
    RUBY MAE MORRISON, age thirteen.
    JOHN SPENCER, age fifteen.
    CLARA SPENCER, age twelve.
    LULU SPENCER, age six.
    LUNDY TAYLOR, age seventeen.

DAVID GRANTLAND, the young minister.
IDA GRANTLAND, David's sister.
MRS. MERCY GRANTLAND, mother of David and Ida.

FAIRLIGHT SPENCER, a mountain woman.
JEB SPENCER, her husband.
(Parents of Christy's students John, Clara, and Lulu.)

DELIA JANE MANNING, a friend of David's from Richmond, Virginia.

PRINCE, black stallion donated to the mission.
GOLDIE, mare belonging to Miss Alice Henderson.

DR. NEIL MACNEILL, the physician of the Cove.

ALICE HENDERSON, a Quaker mission worker from Ardmore, Pennsylvania.

BEN PENTLAND, the mailman.

One

Miz Christy! I got a question to ask you! And it's a matter of life and death—yours!"

Christy Huddleston paused near the edge of Big Spoon Pond. Creed Allen, a nine-year-old who was one of her students at the Cutter Gap Mission school, dashed toward her.

"What is it, Creed?" Christy called. "The Reverend Grantland and I were just about to go for a boat ride."

Creed came to a stop, panting. "I know. That's what I got to ask you about."

"Actually, Creed," David Grantland said with an impatient roll of his dark eyes, "*I* have something to ask Miss Christy, too. Something very important."

Christy looked at David in surprise. Something in his expression sent a shiver through her of excitement mixed with uncertainty. Could it be . . . ?

David had arranged this special evening so carefully. He'd told Christy to dress up, so she'd worn her favorite yellow dress and braided daisies in her sun-streaked hair. David was wearing his Sunday best, and his dark hair was slicked back. They'd had a dinner picnic.

David had brought hand-picked flowers and a homemade cake his sister, Ida, had made especially for the occasion. He'd even brought a candle along in case it got dark. The sun was just now beginning to sink, sending a golden sheen over the pond.

Creed tugged on Christy's arm. His freckled face was tight with worry. "Please, Miz Christy. I need to talk to you, in private. It's for your own good, I reckon."

"David," Christy said, "would you mind giving Creed and me a moment of privacy?"

David sighed loudly. "Creed, do you understand that Miss Christy and I are in the middle of . . ." He hesitated, glancing at Christy. "Of . . . an appointment?"

"Appointment?" Christy teased. "Is that what this is, David?"

"Shucks, Preacher," Creed said apologetically. "I didn't know you was appointin'. I just figgered you was sweetheartin'."

Christy stifled a giggle as David's cheeks turned as red as the setting sun. "Tell me,

Creed," she said, taking the boy aside. "What brings you so far out of your way? What was it you wanted to know?"

"Well . . ." Creed tugged at a ragged overall strap. "It's like this. Can you swim?"

"Yes, I can. But why do you ask?"

Creed lowered his voice to a whisper. "See, me and Sam Houston saw the preacher out here after school, practicin' his boatin'. Now, the preacher's mighty fine at speechifyin', don't get me wrong, but he ain't no boatin' man." Creed glanced at David, then hung his head sadly. "It was like watchin' a hound try to strum a banjo. Just 'cause he tries hard don't mean the Lord meant it to be so."

"Thank you, Creed, for your concern," Christy said, trying very hard not to smile. "But I promise I'll be fine."

"That's a mighty tippy ol' rowboat."

"We are not going to tip over, Creed."

Creed did not look at all convinced.

"Now, you run along," Christy said. "I'll see you on Monday at school."

David was waiting by the boat impatiently. "What was it Creed wanted?"

"He was concerned about my well-being."

"As it happens," David said with a smile, "so am I."

He held out his arm. Christy lifted her long dress and stepped into the little wooden rowboat that belonged to the mission. David gave the boat a gentle push and leapt aboard. The

3

boat rocked back and forth like a huge cradle. He fumbled with the oars for a moment, then settled into an uneven back-and-forth motion.

Christy trailed her hand in the water. The pond was still cold, although the air was surprisingly warm for May. She had only been in the Great Smoky Mountains of Tennessee for a few months, but already Christy had learned that the weather could be very unpredictable.

From far off, a mourning dove cooed its sweet, sad song. Beyond the pond, the mountains loomed—dark and vast, yet somehow comforting. David's oars sent red and gold ripples through the water.

"Sometimes I can't believe how beautiful it is here," Christy whispered. "Fairlight Spencer says it's like God's most perfect painting." Fairlight was Christy's closest friend in Cutter Gap.

David stopped rowing and stared intently at Christy. "Funny," he said softly, "sometimes I feel that way when I look at you, Christy." He reached into his pocket. "There's something I—" He pulled out a white envelope covered with delicate handwriting. "That's not what I was looking for," he muttered. "What *did* I do with that box?"

Christy cleared her throat nervously. Out here alone with David as the first faint stars began to glimmer, she felt very young and awkward. What if David really *was* planning on asking her to marry him? What would she say? She was only nineteen. And they'd only known each other a few months. Was she ready for such a life-changing commitment?

"Who's the letter from?" Christy asked.

"My mother," David said with a grin. "She's coming for a visit soon."

"That will be wonderful!" Christy exclaimed. "I can't wait to meet her."

"Don't be too sure." David gazed up at the darkening sky. "She's a little . . . well, interfering. Especially since my father passed on a couple years ago. She can be rather judgmental, I suppose. But she means well. You know what Ida's like."

Christy smiled. David's sister, Ida, was a stiff, no-nonsense type who took life very seriously.

"Mother's like Ida," David continued, "only she's more outspoken. And she has even higher standards."

"Standards?" Christy asked. "Such as?"

"Such as she thinks her only son should be preaching at a fine city church with velvet cushions on the pews. Not in a schoolhouse filled with people who spit tobacco during his sermons."

"My parents were the same way when I decided to come to Cutter Gap to teach," Christy recalled. "I tried to explain to them that I felt like I had a calling. That there was something I *needed* to do with my life."

"It's not just my work Mother's concerned about." He gave a soft laugh. "She even has a girl picked out for me."

"A girl?" Christy repeated.

"Delia Jane Manning," David said. He looked down at the water, as if he could see her image there. "Very prim, very well-bred. Very boring, too."

"Is she also very pretty?"

"Not to worry, Miss Huddleston. She couldn't hold a candle to you." He took a couple of quick strokes and the rowboat glided to the middle of the pond. It was dark now. The sliver of moon glimmered in the water like a lost smile.

"Did you have 'appointments' with this Miss Manning, too?" Christy teased.

"Oh, we went to some social events together from time to time. Delia loves the opera, the ballet, the theater. And she's a wonderful equestrian."

"That reminds me," Christy said. "Tomorrow you promised me my first jumping lesson on Prince." Prince, the mission's proud black stallion, was a recent donation to the mission.

Christy gave a little shrug. "Of course, it won't exactly be like riding with your friend Miss Manning."

"Thank goodness for that," David said

gently. He leaned closer and reached for Christy's hand. His fingers were trembling. Christy realized that she was trembling, too.

"You know what my mother thinks?" David said. "She thinks I wasn't too happy here at the mission until you came along. She thinks maybe you're the reason I'm staying here."

Christy took a deep breath. "Am I?" she whispered.

David smiled. "What do you think?" He reached into his pocket again and withdrew a small velvet box. Carefully he opened it. "This," he said, "was my great-great-grandmother's." He held out the box. The diamonds caught the moonlight and turned it into a thousand stars.

"Christy," David said, his voice barely audible above the breeze, "may I have your hand—" He stopped suddenly. "No. Wait. This is all wrong. I keep looking into those blue eyes of yours and forgetting all my careful plans." He laughed sheepishly. "I'll bet I've practiced this a hundred times."

Christy felt a strange sensation overtaking her. Dread, fear, joy—what *was* it she was feeling? David was about to ask her to marry him! What should she say? Did she love David? *Really* love him? How did you know such a thing?

Fairlight said love felt like your heart had sprouted wings. "It makes you all fluttery and light inside," she'd promised. Did Christy ever feel that way with David? Sometimes. On the other hand, she'd felt that way with Doctor MacNeill, too, and of *course* she didn't love him!

Still, there was that night at the mission not so long ago. Doctor MacNeill had held her close when they were dancing. Her soaring feelings that evening were still a mystery to her.

Most of the time, all she felt for Neil MacNeill was frustration; the man was so ornery. At least with David, there were no highs or lows. He was just a good, steady, reliable friend. Someone she could always count on.

David made her feel safe and secure. He shared Christy's values. And she had to admit he was very charming, not to mention good-looking. He was the kind of man Christy's mother would have called "a good catch." Wasn't he just the kind of man Christy wanted for a husband?

"David," Christy said. "I'm not sure—"

"Wait, wait," David said. He handed Christy the ring as he shifted his position. The boat began to rock. "I want to do this just right."

Awkwardly, David balanced on one knee. The boat seesawed, sending cold spray into Christy's face.

As she wiped it away, Christy noticed a

dark figure walking along the edge of the pond. "Who could that be?"

"Hello!" came a familiar, deep voice.

"It's the doctor!" Christy cried.

David glanced over his shoulder. "Just my luck," he groaned. "Ignore him, Christy."

"I try to make a habit of it," she joked.

"I mean it. I have something important to say, and I intend to say it now, before I lose my nerve."

"Go ahead, David. I'm listening."

"Christy Rudd Huddleston—" David swallowed, "may I have your hand in marr—"

"How's the fishing, you two?" the doctor called.

David's eyes widened in rage. He clenched his fists, leapt up, and spun around. "Can't you see we're—" he began, but just then the boat began to sway wildly, taking on water with each rock.

Christy grabbed the sides of the rowboat. She watched David flail his arms as he tried to regain his balance. He looked so ridiculous that she began to laugh.

And she kept laughing even as the boat rocked wildly from side to side. Then suddenly the rowboat turned over, and she realized just how cold the water really was.

❧ TWO ❧

Well, well," said Doctor MacNeill as Christy and David struggled onto the shore. "Seems a little chilly for a swim, all things considered."

"We did *not* intend to swim," David muttered as he pulled off a shoe and emptied it of water. "And we wouldn't have had to, if you had just minded your own business!" He turned to Christy. "Are you all right?"

Christy plucked a wet daisy from her hair. Her beautiful dress hung like a wet blanket around her. Her hair was plastered to her face. Realizing what a pitiful sight she must be, she laughed again.

"I'm fine, David, really I am. And you have to admit—" she exchanged a grin with the doctor, "it *is* kind of funny, when you think about it!"

"Our perfect evening is ruined, the mission's

rowboat is submerged, and my only suit is soggy. Forgive me if I fail to see the humor in this."

"Perhaps I can help," Doctor MacNeill offered. "You see, the humor came in right around the time you went flying—"

"What were you doing here, anyway?" David interrupted. "Why aren't you off somewhere healing the sick?"

"I was out for an evening walk, actually," the doctor said. "I ran into Creed Allen awhile back, over past Turkey Ridge. He said he was worried you weren't quite seaworthy. As it turned out, he was right. I thought you were probably trout fishing—not that you'd find anything this time of year. But Creed explained to me you were *appointin'*."

David's mouth tightened into a line. The doctor smiled back with that charming, annoying half-grin of his.

This wasn't the first time Christy had seen the doctor and David at each other's throats. More than one person had told Christy it was because both men were interested in her. But she knew that wasn't the only reason David and Neil didn't get along. David was a young man of God, anxious to change the world. The doctor, on the other hand, had no use for religion. He was older and more cynical. But despite that, he had a charming sense of humor. When Christy was unhappy or confused, she could always count on the doctor to lift her spirits.

She grinned at the two men. David was tall and lean, with dark hair and wide-set brown eyes. The doctor was a big, burly man. His hair was always messy and his clothes were often wrinkled, as if he had better things to worry about. Most of the time, he did. He was the only doctor in the remote mountain cove.

"If you hadn't come along, this night would have been perfect," David seethed. "I had it all planned—"

"Planned?" the doctor interrupted. "Not much planning is needed for a fishing expedition this time of year." He winked at Christy. "I doubt anything was taking the bait. Or should I say anyone?"

Suddenly, Christy gasped. "Oh, no!" she cried. "No!" She grabbed David's arm. "David! The ring! Your great-great-grandmother's diamond ring! I must have dropped it!"

David closed his eyes. He took a deep breath before he spoke. At last he put his arm around Christy's shoulders. "Don't worry," he said wearily. "We'll find it."

"But how?"

"I don't know how. Somehow, it'll turn up. Come on. I'll take you back to the mission house. You'll catch your death out here." With one last glare at Doctor MacNeill, he led Christy away.

As they left, Christy could hear the doctor chuckling behind them. "Diamond ring, eh?" he said. "Strangest bait I ever heard of. Whatever happened to worms?"

— — —

Christy sat on the mission steps the next morning. A dozen children were gathered around her. It was Saturday, and usually the children would have been helping their parents with chores. But word had spread quickly about the reverend's lost diamond ring. Ruby Mae Morrison, a talkative thirteen-year-old who lived at the mission house, had seen to that.

"For sure and certain one of us can find it," Creed vowed. "And the boat, too, like as not."

"That pond's pretty deep, isn't it?" Christy asked doubtfully.

"Nope," said Sam Houston Holcombe, a blond-haired nine-year-old. "Deepest part's maybe seven, eight feet tops."

"Trouble is, the muddy bottom," Ruby Mae said, curling a finger around a lock of red hair thoughtfully. "That ring could be buried. It's soft down there, and squishy-like."

"We'll go a-divin'!" Creed exclaimed. "It's purt-near summer warm today."

"Well, be very careful," Christy warned. "I don't want anyone going near the water who

13

can't swim well." She paused. "Tell you what. I'll give a reward to the person who finds that ring."

"W—what's a re-ward, Teacher?" asked Mountie O'Teale. The shy ten-year-old was overcoming a speech problem with Christy's help.

"It's a present, in a way. A gift for doing something. How about my copy of *Huckleberry Finn*?"

"That would make a right smart re-ward," said Orter Ball, Mountie's older brother. "Even if'n we can't read it all."

"I'll help you with the hard parts," Christy said. Creed nudged Sam Houston.

"Race ya," he said, and a moment later the whole group was rushing for the pond.

Behind Christy, the front door of the mission house opened and Miss Alice Henderson joined her on the porch. "Beautiful morning, isn't it, Miss Alice?" Christy said.

Alice Henderson was a Quaker mission worker from Pennsylvania who had helped start the mission school. She was loved and respected in Cutter Gap and the communities around it. She had a calm, gentle way about her, but she was strong as the old oaks in the mission yard.

"There's an old saying," Miss Alice said, patting Christy on the shoulder. "'There are no accidents.'"

"What do you mean?" Christy asked.

"Losing David's ring that way." Miss Alice gave a knowing smile. "Perhaps it wasn't entirely an accident?"

"Of course it was! David rocked the boat, and it overturned, and that was that."

Miss Alice walked down the steps and examined the buds on a forsythia bush. "I wonder," she said softly, "what you planned to say to David, if you hadn't been so rudely interrupted?"

"Well," Christy said, "I would have told him I was very flattered, and that I cared for him very deeply, and—" She met Miss Alice's deep-set eyes. "And I'd love to stay and talk, Miss Alice, but I have a riding lesson planned. David's teaching me to take Prince over jumps."

"I'll let you off the hook, then," Miss Alice said as Christy started for the pasture. "Just be careful, Christy. Don't take on more than you're ready for."

Christy paused. "Are you talking about riding? Or my romantic life?"

"Both." Miss Alice smiled. "As dangerous as riding can be, romance can be far more painful."

✌ Three ✌

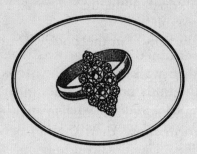

Well, it's good to see you nice and dry again," David called as he trotted across the field on Prince.

Christy laughed. "Maybe next time we should stick to dry land."

"Does that mean you intend for there to be a next time?" David dismounted gracefully and reached for Christy's hand. "I never did get an answer to my question, Christy."

Christy pulled her hand away, tucking a stray piece of hair behind her ear. "Actually, I don't think you ever finished your question."

David hesitated. "Somehow, this doesn't seem like quite the right time or place—" He was interrupted by a loud, impatient snort from Prince.

"Prince seems to agree," Christy said. She stroked the black stallion's silky mane. "I guess he's anxious for our lesson to start."

"I suppose it can wait. Besides, it's hard to propose without a ring."

"I'm so sorry about that, David. I feel like it's all my fault."

"Don't be silly. I'm the one who tipped the boat."

"Some of the children are diving for the ring right now. I said I'd give them a reward if they found it. A copy of *Huckleberry Finn*."

"It's worth more than that in sentimental value alone," David said grimly.

"I know." Christy patted his back. "But it's bound to turn up. The pond's pretty shallow."

David helped Christy into the saddle and she settled into place. She'd learned to ride as a little girl, but that was always side-saddle, on gentle, well-trained horses. Since the mission had acquired Prince, Christy had become determined to improve her riding skills. She still felt strange, riding like the men did. But after watching Ruby Mae win a recent horse race, Christy had realized that she could never control a powerful stallion like Prince while riding sidesaddle.

To make things easier, Christy had cut one of her skirts down the middle, then sewn up the split to make what amounted to a pair of very loose trousers. She felt very daring wearing them. Back home in Asheville, North Carolina, they would have caused a scandal. But here in the Tennessee mountains, women often wore men's trousers—for practical reasons, or because they were so poor they simply wore whatever they could get their hands on.

"All right," David called, "let's start by getting warmed up. Take him around the field a few times at an easy trot."

Christy gave Prince a gentle nudge. He responded instantly, trotting her around the field in graceful arcs. He was such a powerful animal, she couldn't help being a little afraid. But she reminded herself that if her students could ride this way, so could she. Besides, jumping was a skill that could come in handy here in the mountains. When she was tending to the sick, Miss Alice often rode her horse, Goldie, to remote areas. Knowing how to take small jumps was important, since there were plenty of creeks and downed trees to get around.

"How about a gallop?" David suggested.

Prince obliged by flying across the field. Christy's heart leapt at his speed. But once she let herself relax into the rolling movement of Prince's gait, she felt thrilled. She smiled at David as she passed him. He was watching her with that look he so often had around her—part admiration, part affection, part confusion.

Suddenly she recalled Miss Alice's question. What *would* Christy have said, if things had turned out differently last night? She imagined saying the words. *Yes, David, I accept your proposal.* She imagined walking down the aisle of the mission church wearing a long white dress—maybe her mother's wedding dress. *And do you, Christy Rudd Huddleston, take this man to be your lawfully wedded husband?*

"Miz Christy!"

Christy turned in her saddle. Creed and Ruby Mae and several other students had gathered by the fence. Their torn, oversized clothes were soaking wet, and their hair hung in damp strings.

"Any luck?" Christy called.

"Nope," Creed reported as Prince came to a stop near the fence. "Not a lick."

"It's awful muddy, Miz Christy," Sam Houston added as he tried to wring out his overalls. "Like tryin' to find a needle in a haystack."

"We'll keep a-lookin', though," Creed vowed. "We just come on over to see your jumpin' lesson."

"Ain't he just the nicest horse you ever laid eyes on, Miz Christy?" Ruby Mae asked as she perched on the fence. She leaned over and planted a big kiss on Prince's muzzle.

"Aw, don't go a-slobberin' all over a fine animal such as that," Creed moaned.

"He's a-goin' to need a bath for sure now," Sam Houston agreed.

With a laugh, Christy nudged Prince back

into a trot. In the center of the field, David had positioned a small jump made of two crossed pine logs.

"Now, the important thing to remember about jumping is that you don't want to get in the way of the horse," David instructed. "Let him do all the work. You're just the passenger."

Christy smiled. "Easy for you to say."

"Hey, I'm not exactly the world's greatest equestrian—"

"No," Christy interrupted, "Delia is."

"I hope the fact that you're bringing her up can be interpreted as a sign of jealousy."

"I just have a very good memory," Christy replied.

"The point is, I'm just telling you the basics."

"That's all I need," Christy said. "Enough to get around these mountains when I have to."

"What I want you to do is take Prince around the field again, nice and easy. Then get a good, straight-on approach to this jump, lean forward, and give Prince lots of rein. He'll do the rest."

Christy took a deep breath. Suddenly, this did not seem like such a good idea. She could see herself tumbling off Prince, doing endless somersaults all the way back to the mission house. It could be very humiliating. Not to mention painful.

"Don't worry, Miz Christy," Ruby Mae called. "It ain't hard, I promise."

On the other hand, it could be equally humiliating to fail at something so simple—something most of her students had been doing since they could walk.

"You won't fall," David said. "I'm looking out for you."

With a grim smile, Christy took Prince around the field. The children applauded as she passed them. "Pretend you're a-flyin'!" Ruby Mae called, and Christy took her advice. She took a deep breath, then another, as Prince approached the little jump.

"Give him rein!" David called.

Suddenly they were there. For a split second, the sound of Prince's thundering hooves vanished, and all Christy could hear was the whoosh of air as they soared over the logs.

The landing was harder. Christy had to grab a handful of mane for extra support. But as she turned back to see David's proud smile, she realized that she'd actually managed her first, official jump.

Ruby Mae let out an ear-splitting whistle. "Atta girl, Miz Christy!"

Christy slowed Prince to a walk. "Well, Teacher?" she asked David.

"Nice work. Very nice. Want to try again?"

Christy nodded. With one jump under her belt, she felt certain the next one would be easier. Again she took Prince around the field. As she neared the children, they applauded.

"You two just flew like a big bird right over that jump!" Ruby Mae called.

Christy waved, then set her eyes on the logs. This wasn't so bad, after all. Her fears seemed silly now. Maybe she would take it a little faster this time—

Suddenly, Prince let out a horrified whinny of protest. He reared back on his hind legs as Christy clung to the saddle, desperately trying to hang on.

"Snake!" one of the children screamed. "Prince is spooked!"

"Hang on, Miz Christy!" Ruby Mae cried, but already Christy could feel her grip slipping.

David was running toward her. "Hang on!" he cried.

"I'm . . . I'm trying," Christy managed. She could sense the huge horse's terrible fear.

Prince lowered his front legs for a moment, and Christy caught a glimpse of a black snake sliding out from a nearby rock. It was just a harmless little black snake, but Prince didn't know that. He let out another terrified, anguished whinny. Again he reared back with even more force, and this time Christy could not hold on.

As she went flying backward through the air, she heard Ruby Mae's screams and David's cries, and then suddenly the world went completely black.

❧ Four ❧

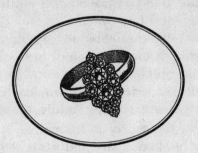

I*s she a-comin' to?"*

"She's movin' some. That be a good sign, don't it, Doctor?"

"That's some bump Teacher's got on her head, ain't it?"

"Christy? Can you hear me?"

Christy tried to focus on the voices floating through her head. Was that Doctor MacNeill's voice she'd heard?

"Christy? It's Neil. Don't try to move too suddenly. You took quite a spill. You've been unconscious for the last hour or so."

Christy moved toward the sound of his voice.

Pain ripped through her head. Her left temple felt raw.

She tried to open her eyes, but there was something covering them—something cool and moist. She reached to touch it.

23

"That's a cold cloth, dear." It was Miss Alice. "To help keep down the swelling."

A gentle hand removed the cloth. Slowly Christy opened her eyes.

At least, she *thought* she'd opened them.

"The cloth," she whispered, her voice filled with panic, "take off the—"

She felt a steadying hand on her shoulder. "Be still, now," Doctor MacNeill said. She could hear the worry in his voice.

Christy blinked, again and again. Up, down, up, down. There was no difference.

"I can't see!" she cried in terror. She lurched upright and reached out her hands. Where were all her friends? Their voices were so close, but where were *they*?

Her right hand landed on a shoulder, and a warm, strong hand grabbed her fingers. "Don't panic," came the doctor's soothing voice.

"Of course she's panicked." It was David. He sounded frantic. "What's happened to her, Doctor?"

"Calm down, Reverend. It's probably just temporary." The doctor's voice grew softer. "You took a nasty spill off that horse, Christy. Lie back down now, and let me take a look."

Reluctantly, Christy let herself be lowered back down to her pillow.

"Cain't she see nothin' a-tall?"

Christy recognized the little whispered voice as Mountie's. The children were probably just as terrified as she was.

"I'm fine, Mountie," Christy said, forcing cheer into her voice. She reached out her hand and Mountie grabbed it.

"You sure, Teacher?" Mountie whispered.

"Isn't Doctor MacNeill the best doctor in Cutter Gap?" Christy asked.

"Well, I reckon," Mountie said. "Course he's the *only* doctor."

"Come on, children," Miss Alice said firmly. "Let's let the doctor do his job."

"But what if she needs us?" Creed asked.

"She won't be needing you any time soon," the doctor said irritably.

Christy winced at his tone. "You go on, children. See if you can find that ring for me, all right?"

As the children were leaving, Christy lowered her voice. "Tell me the truth, Neil. Why can't I see?"

"First let's decide just how much you can't see. How many fingers am I holding up?"

Christy gazed straight ahead. Her head throbbed. She saw nothing but a vast dark mist. "Thirteen?"

"In other words, you can see nothing."

"It's just emptiness. Like a dark, foggy night."

The doctor sighed deeply. Christy heard some whispering and shuffling, followed by sounds she couldn't quite identify. Fresh air rushed past. Someone had opened the windows in her room.

A few moments later, the doctor returned to her bedside. "I want you to turn your head and body just slightly to the right. Do you see anything?"

Christy did as he instructed. Every inch of movement caused a sharp stab of pain to her temple. She waited. The room was hushed. She could feel the gentle touch of the early afternoon sun on her arms.

She could *feel* its brightness. But she could not see it.

"Nothing," she admitted at last.

Again, the long sigh. "All right, then," said the doctor. "One more thing."

She heard him moving. She could tell he was close by the sweet smell of his tobacco. In the background she heard footsteps marching back and forth, back and forth. Was that David, pacing?

"Look straight ahead for me," the doctor instructed.

Christy did. Darkness stretched before her like a black quilt.

She waited, and then the sharp smell of kerosene met her nose. On one edge of the darkness, something changed. It was as if she were seeing the first faint glimmerings of dawn.

"Anything?" the doctor asked in a calm, steady voice.

"It's . . . it's as if the sun is coming up,"

Christy began. "No, not that strong. But I saw something. Movement, light . . . *something*."

"Then she'll see again!" David cried.

"Not so fast, Reverend," the doctor said. "It's a good sign, but that's all. Just a sign."

"The doctor was moving a lantern very close to your eyes," said Miss Alice. "That was the light you perceived."

"What does that mean?" Christy asked, almost afraid to hope.

Doctor MacNeill took her hand. "Here's what we know, Christy. And I'm no eye specialist, mind you. You've taken a bad fall. When Prince threw you, you hit your head on a sharp rock. There's a lot of damage to the eye and temple area—cuts, bruises, that sort of thing. But that doesn't explain the loss of sight. That could be caused by swelling from your concussion. There may be pressure on the optic nerve."

"So when the swelling goes down," David interrupted, "then she'll be able to see again?"

"Could be," the doctor said cautiously. "But the swelling may have caused permanent damage. We can only wait and hope. I've only seen a couple other cases like this. And they didn't . . . well, they didn't turn out well."

Silence fell. Christy let the words sink in, one by one.

The swelling may have caused permanent

damage. Permanent damage meant she might be blind.

Blind. Forever.

"Meantime," the doctor continued, "I'm going to bandage up those cuts around your eyes and temple to keep them from getting infected." He paused. "Is there a lot of pain?"

Christy smiled. "Yes. In my hand, actually. You're squeezing it too hard."

"Sorry about that."

"How long . . . how long till we know something?" Christy asked. "For sure, I mean."

"It's hard to say. A few weeks, most likely. Maybe even sooner."

"There must be something we can do!" David exploded.

"There is, David," Miss Alice said gently. "We can pray."

"I'm not a praying man myself," the doctor said. "But if I were, now would be the time I'd try it."

The others left while Doctor MacNeill bandaged Christy's eyes.

"Neil?" she asked in a whisper when he was done. "One thing. I was just wondering . . . is it all right if I—"

"What?"

Christy let out a soft sob.

Doctor MacNeill touched her hair tenderly. "It's all right," he said, his voice breaking. "You go right ahead and cry."

❧ Five ❧

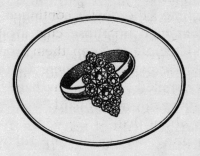

May I come in?"

At the sound of David's voice, Christy stirred. The world was black. She tried to open her eyes, but something heavy made it impossible. Her head stung as she sat up. Gingerly she touched the thick cotton bandages Doctor MacNeill had placed around her head.

"It's me. David."

"I know. I can still hear," Christy snapped. Then, her voice softening, she added, "I'm sorry, David. I didn't mean to sound that way."

"You have every right to sound that way," David said. Christy heard the sound of dishes on a tray. The scent of peppermint tea drifted past.

"Ida fixed you a tray," David explained. "I'll put it here, on your nightstand."

"I'm starving. Tell Miss Ida thanks."

"Here. I'll hand you the cup." David placed the steaming cup of tea into Christy's hands.

Carefully Christy lifted the cup. The hot steam drifted past her chin. She put the china edge to her lips and started to take a sip, but she'd misjudged how full the cup was. Hot tea dribbled down her chin.

"What a mess," she groaned. "You'd think I could manage a cup of tea!"

"Don't worry," David said. "Here's a napkin."

Christy's lower lip quivered. "It's such a simple thing," she said. "Drinking a cup of tea. You never even give it a second thought, but now . . ."

"No use crying over spilled tea," David tried to joke.

"How am I ever going to do all the things I used to do?" Christy asked, trying not to sob. "Teaching, for example. How can I manage the children? I can't even drink a cup of tea. How can I grade a paper or write on the blackboard?"

David was silent for a moment. "The truth is, I don't know, Christy. But if anyone can do it, you can."

"You have more faith in me than I do," she replied.

"I feel so . . ." David took a ragged breath. "This is all my fault, Christy. I was the one who was teaching you to jump. I was the one who promised you nothing would happen."

Christy could hear the pain in his voice. "David, that's crazy. Prince saw a snake. He threw me. That's all. It wasn't your fault in any way."

"There's something I have to say to you," David said. He cleared his throat. "I know this isn't the right time, and I know you probably can't answer me. But I still want you to marry me, Christy. With all my heart I want that. Nothing's changed."

"Oh, David," Christy whispered, "*everything's* changed."

"I love you, Christy Huddleston. I love your good heart and your spirit and the way you laugh. It doesn't matter to me one whit whether you can see or not." He gave a soft laugh. "Truth is, it might be an advantage. I'm not the handsomest catch in the world, after all."

"I have the feeling a lot of women would disagree with that."

"So?"

Christy fingered the edge of her blanket. "David, I need time. Time to think about everything that's happened, and time to sort out my feelings—"

"You're not sure how you feel about me, then?"

"I'm not sure how I feel about *any*thing," Christy said lightly.

"Is there . . . someone else?"

"You know there's no one else."

"Well, I hope not, but you never know. Sometimes I wonder if the Doctor . . ." David's voice trailed off.

"David, please. Neil MacNeill is the most aggravating man I've ever known. He's pig-headed and arrogant and—" Christy stopped herself. "Well, you needn't worry there."

"Good," David said, but he didn't sound entirely convinced. "Well, anyway. I'll give you all the time you need, Christy. I just wanted you to know that my offer stands— ring or no ring."

"You never know. Miracles do happen. Maybe the ring will show up," said Christy.

"Miracles *do* happen. You remember that, all right?"

Christy heard a soft knock at the door, then a familiar voice. "How's the patient?" Miss Alice asked.

"The patient's turning out to be quite a slob," Christy said. "I can't even drink a cup of tea without it turning into a disaster."

"I should let the patient get some rest." David leaned down and kissed Christy on her cheek. "Sleep well."

When he was gone, Miss Alice sat on the edge of Christy's bed. She smelled of pine and balsam and fresh air, as if she'd brought the mountains straight into Christy's bedroom.

Christy had always found it calming to be in Miss Alice's presence. She had such a sense of serenity and grace about her. But tonight, as the dark pressed in on Christy, she felt as if no one could console her—not even Miss Alice.

"Is there anything I can bring you?" Miss Alice asked.

"Some light would be nice."

Miss Alice laughed gently. She reached over toward Christy's nightstand, then took Christy's hand.

Christy recognized the soft leather binding. "My Bible."

"You asked for light. And there it is."

Her tone was both soothing and direct, as it always was. There was no hint of pity. Somehow, knowing that Miss Alice did not intend to treat her any differently reassured Christy.

"Miss Alice," Christy asked, "why did this have to happen now? To me?"

"You're not the first to have her strength tested. And you won't be the last."

"I know that." Christy swallowed back a sob. "But I feel like I was just starting to develop a relationship with the children, to get them to trust an outsider. Now all that's ruined. There was so much I wanted to do here."

"So do it."

"But . . . but I can't! Not now. Not this way."

"Why not?"

The question was so blunt, Christy paused. *Why not?* Wasn't it obvious? How could Miss Alice be so cruel?

"Because I'm blind!" Christy blurted. "Because I may be blind forever, Miss Alice!"

Her words echoed in the little room. Miss Alice sat calmly and quietly. Quakers were fond of silences. They were as much a part of Miss Alice's conversations as words.

"There are many teachers," Miss Alice said at last, "who would look at the one-room schoolhouse in which you teach, and the sixty-seven children, and the poverty and superstition and ignorance, and they would say they could never teach with such handicaps. They would tell you it was impossible. You, of course, did not look at the situation that way. Some see a glass as half-empty. Others see it as half-full."

"But to teach without being able to see . . ." Christy gave a shuddering sigh. "I can get by without paper or pencils. I can't get by without sight."

"You may not be able to teach in the same way," Miss Alice said. "And you most certainly will have to learn to rely on others for help. But then, we all must ask for help from time to time."

"I can't do it," Christy whispered. "I just know I'll never teach again."

"Perhaps not right away. But you will

teach again, when you are ready. The Lord does not give us more than we can handle, Christy." With a gentle hug, Miss Alice left the room.

Christy ran her fingers over her Bible as Miss Alice's words lingered in her ears. Blind, she wasn't going to be the same person she'd been. Miss Alice was wrong. There was no way that Christy could ever teach again.

What would she do instead? She could go home. Back to safe, secure Asheville, where her parents would take care of her. But then what? What would she do with her life? She thought back to that day last summer at the church retreat where she'd first heard about the need for teachers in the Great Smoky Mountains. Something deep in her heart had told her that she'd found the place where she belonged. Teaching here in Cutter Gap, she'd felt certain, was her calling. But how could it be now?

Christy fumbled for her nightstand. She nearly knocked over her plate of untouched toast before her hand grazed her little diary. Her pen was tucked inside. It took several more minutes for her to find her inkpot and prepare to write. At last the diary was perched on her lap. She opened to the last page she'd written in, marked with a silk ribbon. At the top of the page, she began to write. Each letter she wrote with great care, slowly and evenly, imagining the lines and curves in her mind. She felt like one of her students practicing penmanship.

Saturday, May 4, 1912

The Lord does not give us more than we can handle.

Christy paused, her head tilted down, her bandaged eyes aimed toward words she could not see. She tried to make them come alive on the page. She tried to hear Miss Alice's confident tone as she'd spoken them. But in her heart, Christy knew that they were smudged scribblings, and nothing more.

❧ Six ❧

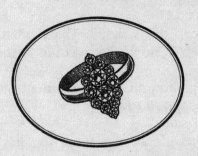

Miz Christy! What are you doing out of bed?" Christy was dressed and sitting on the edge of the bed combing her hair.

"It's Sunday morning, Ruby Mae," Christy said calmly. "I'm getting ready for church."

Christy heard the clatter of dishes. The smoky scent of bacon filled the room. Ruby Mae must have brought up a breakfast tray. Well, that was very thoughtful. But Christy intended to eat downstairs in the dining room, just like she always did. She could at least manage that much.

"Did I hear you right? Did you say church, Miz Christy?"

"Yes. Church. You remember—sermons, hymns, prayers?"

The bed bounced as Ruby Mae plopped down near Christy. "I don't see how you can go to church," Ruby Mae said earnestly. "I mean, seein' as how you're in a cap that's dated."

"I'm *what*?"

"In a cap that's dated. That's what Miz Ida says you are now. On account of not seein' nothin'."

Christy thought for a moment. "Oh! You mean *incapacitated*."

"Like I said."

"Well, if it's all the same to Miss Ida, I'll decide what I can and cannot do. And I'm going to have breakfast downstairs, then go to church. After all, I got dressed all by myself this morning. It took nearly a half-hour, but I did it." Christy stood. "As you can see, I'm ready."

"Well . . ." Ruby Mae hesitated. "I don't mean to be a botheration, Miz Christy. But you ain't *exactly* ready."

"Why? What's wrong?"

"Well, to begin with, your skirt's all turned which-a-ways. And your colors are kinda . . . colorful."

"You mean they don't match?"

"I guess that all depends. I mean, the colors in a rainbow don't rightly match up, neither. But when you look at them together-like, it's a heap of purtiness just the same."

Christy dropped onto the bed with a sigh. She'd awakened this morning feeling determined to make the best of things. But what could she possibly accomplish in this world if she couldn't even manage to get dressed by herself?

"Don't you worry yourself none, Miz Christy," Ruby Mae said firmly. "I'll git you fixed up as purty as a spring rose."

"Thanks, Ruby Mae. I guess I need more help than I thought."

Ruby Mae bustled about the room. "Now, I ain't no fashionable city-gal, but I figger these look church-right." She placed a pile of clothes in Christy's lap.

"Thanks," Christy said quietly, wondering if she should trust Ruby Mae's fashion tastes. "When I've changed, will you help me down the stairs so I can have breakfast?"

"Yes'm." A long silence followed. Somehow, Christy could feel Ruby Mae's intense dark gaze on her.

"Miz Christy?" Ruby Mae said at last. "Can I ask you somethin'? Somethin' personal-like?"

"Of course."

"What's it like? Bein' blind, I mean?"

"I'm not blind, Ruby Mae," Christy said sharply. She took a deep breath. "What I mean is, I'm not sure that this is permanent. Doctor MacNeill says that when the swelling goes down, I may be as good as new."

Ruby Mae reached for Christy's hand and gave it a shy squeeze. "I hope so, Miz Christy.

Truly I do. And I'm sorry I asked such a fool question."

"It wasn't foolish, Ruby Mae. The truth is, it's hard to describe what it's like not to see. You know how it is when you look down the well in the mission yard? How the dark just seems to go on and on forever? It's like that, a little."

"Lookin' down that well gives me the cold shivers."

Christy sighed. "Me, too," she said softly.

A few minutes later, Ruby Mae led Christy down the stairs. Even holding onto Ruby Mae's arm, every step felt like a gamble. It was like walking off a cliff while wearing a blindfold. Being so helpless was a strange and awful feeling. Christy was Ruby Mae's teacher. Yet here she was, being dressed and guided by her thirteen-year-old student.

At the bottom of the stairs, Christy heard the clink of silverware. The sharp smell of coffee wafted past.

"Christy!" Miss Alice exclaimed from the direction of the dining room. "How wonderful to see you, dear." A moment later, she was at Christy's side, helping her to the table. "Do you feel up to this?"

"I'm fine, really I am," Christy insisted as she sat down in her usual spot.

"She got dressed all by herself," Ruby Mae announced.

Christy fumbled for her napkin. "Actually, I required a little fashion advice."

"Are you sure you should be up so soon?" David asked.

"I fixed a fine breakfast tray," Miss Ida said. "It doesn't seem right, you walking around like this."

"Would you all stop fussing?" Christy demanded. "I'm having breakfast, that's all. It's not like I'm trying to climb Mount Everest, or—" she paused, "or teach school."

"Christy's right," Miss Alice said. "It's her decision."

A chair scraped on the wooden floor. "I'll start another plate of eggs," Miss Ida said.

"I'm sorry to be such a bother," Christy apologized.

"Not at all," Miss Ida said, putting a comforting hand on Christy's shoulder. "Anything I can do, you just ask."

It was all Christy could do to keep from crying. Miss Ida was usually so gruff! The pity in her voice was almost more than Christy could bear. But perhaps she was going to have to get used to the pity of others.

Breakfast was an ordeal. Christy insisted on doing everything herself, which meant that half her scrambled eggs ended up in her lap. She was only slightly more successful with her toast.

She was almost done eating when Doctor

MacNeill entered the mission house. "What on earth are you doing out of bed?" he demanded as he strode into the dining room.

"Making a huge mess of the breakfast table," Christy replied.

"I want you to go straight back up to your room," the doctor said, sounding furious. He knelt beside Christy and examined her bandages. "Any dizziness? Nausea?"

"I feel perfectly fine."

"Pain?"

"My head still hurts some. But not much, I promise." Christy crossed her arms over her chest. "And there's no use arguing with me, Neil. I am going to church."

"I can't allow that," the doctor said. "You've had too much trauma. You need to rest for several days."

"You look like *you* need to rest, Neil," Miss Alice said. "You may not have heard, but there's a new-fangled idea floating around these parts. We call it 'sleep.'"

"I was up all night reading medical books." Doctor MacNeill pulled up a chair. "I was hoping . . . well, I just wanted to be sure there wasn't anything I'd missed."

"What did you find out?" Christy asked as she struggled to locate her glass of juice.

"There are cases of sight recovery after concussion. And then there are other cases . . ." The doctor's voice trailed off. "We'll just have to wait and see," he said simply.

"And pray," David added.

"Thank you, Neil," Christy said. "Thank you for trying. Now go home and get some sleep."

"That is, unless you'd care to join us in church, Doctor," David said. "There's always room for one more."

"Not for a wayward soul like me," the doctor said. "I can't talk you out of this, Christy?"

"I need to go, Neil. I can't explain it. I just know I'll feel better there."

"Well, I can see I'm outnumbered." The doctor pushed back his chair. "I'll check on you again soon."

"I'll keep an eye on her," Miss Alice said.

"And tomorrow at school, I'll watch out for her like a mama hen with her chicks," Ruby Mae vowed.

David cleared his throat. No one spoke. Someone—Miss Ida, probably—began clearing up the dishes, one by one.

Christy knew what they were thinking—there wasn't going to be school tomorrow, at least not with Christy teaching.

"Why's everybody so all-fired tongue-tied all of a sudden?" Ruby Mae demanded.

"We're going to have to wait and see about school, Ruby Mae," David explained.

"Christy is in no condition to teach," the doctor added.

Again, Christy felt the pity flowing around her, tugging at her like an ocean current. It was as if, in the space of one terrible moment, she'd lost the person she was. She wasn't Miss Christy Huddleston, teacher, anymore. She was just another helpless somebody to whisper about.

Who could blame them? The truth was, she felt sorry for herself, too.

She started to sob. Just as she pushed back her chair to leave, she heard someone knocking at the mission's front door. "Preacher?" someone called. "It's Ben Pentland."

"Mr. Pentland!" David exclaimed. "Is this about the service today? Or have you taken to delivering mail on Sundays?"

"It ain't mail I be deliverin'. I done brought you a visitor—"

"And I must say it was the most uncomfortable buggy ride of my life!" came a high-pitched, woman's voice.

"Mother?" David cried.

"David, sweetie pie!"

Seven

Christy heard the swish of petticoats as Mrs. Grantland rushed to embrace David.

"*Sweetie*-pie?" Doctor MacNeill whispered loudly.

"But I thought you weren't coming until next week!" David said, sounding a little shocked.

"I changed plans. I knew you wouldn't mind," Mrs. Grantland said briskly.

"Well, welcome to our humble abode," David said.

"Humble, indeed! I've seen outhouses with more style." Mrs. Grantland clapped her hands. "Ida, dear girl, come here and give your mother a kiss."

"It's good to see you, Mother," Miss Ida said.

"What have you done to yourselves? You

both look positively rural." Mrs. Grantland clucked her tongue. "Aren't you going to introduce me to your friends?"

"I'm Alice Henderson, Mrs. Grantland. It's a great pleasure to meet you at last."

"Oh, yes. The missionary woman from Pennsylvania," Mrs. Grantland said. She did not sound altogether impressed.

"I'm Neil MacNeill, Mrs. Grantland," said the doctor.

"And this—" Mrs. Grantland gasped. "Don't tell me this is Miss Huddleston, the one you've written me so much about?"

"Oh, no'm. I'm Ruby Mae Morrison."

Mrs. Grantland gave a relieved sigh. "Ah, yes. David mentioned you in his letters."

"Proud to meet you," Ruby Mae said. "I never rightly figgered the preacher *had* a mama. But I guess everybody does, even preachers—"

"Yes, well, delighted to meet you," Mrs. Grantland interrupted. "And who might this unfortunate soul be?"

Christy realized with a start that Mrs. Grantland must be referring to her.

"This," David said, "is Christy Huddleston, Mother."

Christy extended her hand out into the air, but Mrs. Grantland didn't take it. "It's nice to meet you, Mrs. Grantland. David's told me so much about you."

"Is she *blind*?" Mrs. Grantland asked David, as if Christy were deaf as well.

"Christy had an accident, Mother," David said tensely. "She can't see, but we're all praying that it's just temporary."

"Oh, my. Poor dear. What a shame."

Christy felt a hand patting her on the head. Suddenly she felt the need for air. "We were just on our way to church, Mrs. Grantland," she said as she stood. "Will you be joining us?"

"I was hoping to freshen up first. Not that it would matter much here," Mrs. Grantland added with a dry laugh. "The church—would that be the wooden building I noticed on the way in?"

"It's the schoolhouse as well," Miss Alice said. "David built most of it himself, from the ground up."

"He always was a talented boy."

"Indeed," the doctor muttered under his breath.

Mr. Pentland cleared his throat. "There's a couple big trunks out yonder."

"I'll help you with them," David volunteered.

"Me, too," Ida said.

"I'd better supervise." Mrs. Grantland rushed off, skirts swishing.

"Is she gone?" Christy asked in a whisper.

"Yep," Doctor MacNeill said in a low voice. "She's not one to mince words, is she?"

"David warned us she could be rather blunt," Miss Alice said. "Now I see what he meant. Of course, she's probably very tired after her long trip."

"I thought she was kinda mean about Miz Christy and all," Ruby Mae said.

Christy sighed. "I could use a little fresh air. Doctor, would you mind escorting me over to the church?"

"As long as you don't ask me to stay," the doctor joked.

Christy took his arm and they headed out into the sunshine. She could hear Mrs. Grantland's voice on the far side of the mission house, directing David to be careful with her bags. She could hear the squeak of the springs in Mr. Pentland's wagon, and the babble of the mockingbirds in the nearby oak tree.

Christy paused near a stand of pines. She rested her hand on one of the trees and held up her head toward the sun. "Do you think I'll ever see the sky again, Neil?" she whispered.

"I hope so, Christy. With all my heart, I hope so."

They stood for a moment, arms linked. Mrs. Grantland's harsh voice floated over the breeze.

You can't possibly be thinking of marrying her now, David.

Christy clutched Doctor MacNeill's arm tighter. "She's talking about me!"

"Come on," he said. "You don't need to be hearing this."

But Christy stood firm. She could hear David replying in hushed tones. Then she heard Mrs. Grantland again.

But she's blind, David. What kind of a wife would a blind woman make?

Christy's heart seemed to stop. Mrs. Grantland was right, of course. What kind of wife would Christy make now? What kind of teacher? What kind of *person*?

Miss Alice had been wrong to encourage Christy last night. She'd just been trying to be kind. Mrs. Grantland was only saying what everyone else was thinking.

Doctor MacNeill pulled Christy along toward the church. "Ignorant old crow," he muttered. "You'd make a fine wife for any man. I hope you know that." He gave a short laugh. "Well, not *any* man. Not the Reverend, certainly."

"And why not David?"

"You're a fine woman, Christy. You don't have to settle for less. Remember that when you answer the Reverend. Don't make a choice you'll regret the rest of your life because . . . because you're selling yourself short now."

Christy was surprised when his voice broke.

He led her up the stairs to the schoolhouse and helped her settle on a front bench. Then he left without another word.

— — —

Church was a new experience. Without being able to see, it became a picture made of sounds and sensations and scents. It was the familiar smell of chalk and wood smoke and tobacco. It was the sound of rustling Sunday school papers and the coos of babies and the whispers of restless children. It was the vibration in the wooden floor, as the congregation tapped their feet while singing an old hymn.

Oh, for a faith that will not shrink, they sang, and Christy listened to their voices surround her like a warm embrace. Here, with her mountain friends, she felt safe and secure. One by one as they'd entered the church this morning, they'd come to her. The children had climbed in her lap and hugged her. The women had brought her cakes and cookies and breads—things they could hardly afford to give away. The men had been more awkward, but they, too, had come forward. Their words were simple—*Powerful sorry to hear about your troubles, Miz Christy*, or *I done prayed for you last night*. But what she'd heard in their voices wasn't pity. It wasn't anything like the tone she'd heard in Mrs. Grantland's harsh words. It was love.

When the room grew hushed, Christy knew that David was about to start his sermon. She heard his steady footsteps as he walked to the small pulpit.

"The preacher's a-comin," whispered Mountie, who was sitting next to Christy on the hard wooden bench. She was serving as an extra pair of eyes for Christy, informing her about what was happening in the room.

"That's my son," Christy heard Mrs. Grantland whisper in a pew behind her.

The memory of her hurtful words came back to Christy. *You can't possibly be thinking of marrying her now, David.*

They were strong, blunt words. Words that stung. At first, they had made Christy want to cry. But now, surrounded by her friends, she began to feel angry.

What kind of a wife would a blind woman make?

"Hebrews, 11:1," David began in his clear, strong voice. "'Faith is the substance of things hoped for, the evidence of things not seen.'" He paused. "'The evidence of things not seen.' What does that mean? What does that mean to each of us as we struggle through the trials of life?"

Christy listened intently. Somehow she felt as if David were speaking directly to her.

"There are many ways of seeing," he continued. "We can see with our eyes, of course. But that doesn't begin to paint the whole picture. Even the most perfect, shiny apple can have a worm inside. So how else can we see?"

Christy heard steps, and she knew that David was moving down the aisle that separated the men and women. He liked to move among the congregation as he spoke to them.

"We can 'see' with our other senses, too," David continued. "We can hear and smell and taste and touch, but we're never going to know the true nature of a thing that way. Sight can blur. Hearing can go bad. You have only to look at Jeb Spencer's old coon dog, Magic, to know that. Jeb tells me that hound couldn't sniff out a skunk in a patch of pokeweed." The room broke into laughter. "No, only the heart can detect the evidence of things not seen."

He paused. Christy could tell he was only a few feet away, near the end of her bench.

"We cannot touch faith. We can't see it with our eyes, or hear it with our ears. But we can know it, as sure and solid as the earth beneath our feet, if we use our hearts." David's voice wavered. "You don't need eyes to have faith. You don't need anything but a good and loving and open heart."

Christy felt Mountie's small fingers lace into hers. When Christy had started teaching, Mountie had barely spoken more than a few garbled words. She'd had a terrible speech problem, and the taunts of her classmates had left her almost mute. But a tiny gesture of caring from Christy—sewing a few old buttons onto Mountie's worn and tattered coat—had been the beginning of a miraculous change.

"We can see the world in a whole new way," David said softly, "when we use our hearts, instead of our eyes."

Soon the room was full of song again. *Amazing grace*, they sang, in that boisterous, full-of-life way they had. Christy sang, too, letting the words move her.

Slowly, other words came back to her— Miss Alice's words. *You will teach again, when you are ready.*

For the first time since her accident, Christy felt a glimmer of hope. What kind of a wife would she make? What kind of teacher? What kind of person?

She wasn't sure, but she knew she wanted to find out.

❧ Eight ❧

I must say that was a fine sermon," Mrs. Grantland said that evening at the dinner table. "Although the circumstances left a great deal to be desired. I don't know how you do it, David, dear. The primitive conditions! I mean, really. *Pigs* living under the floor!"

"Them's hogs, Miz Grantland," Ruby Mae corrected.

"Thank you for clearing that up."

Christy smiled. All through dinner, Mrs. Grantland had been talking that way. Poor David! Christy didn't know how he managed to keep his tongue. The only time he'd lashed out was when Mrs. Grantland had suggested Christy might be more "comfortable" eating in her room, where she could make a mess without being embarrassed.

It hadn't even bothered Christy. Ever since

church that morning, she'd been filled with a sense of hope and resolve.

"And the *smells*!" Mrs. Grantland continued. "I thought I was going to faint. Thank goodness I had my perfumed hankie with me."

"You get used to it after a while, Mother," Miss Ida said.

"Goodness, me! I certainly hope not, dear. I keep telling David he needs a ministry back home in Richmond. He belongs in a big, fine church with a congregation that understands what he's saying. A church without any tobacco spitting or mangy dogs or pigs."

"Hogs, ma'am," Ruby Mae corrected again.

"The congregation here may not be the best dressed or the most educated, Mrs. Grantland," said Miss Alice, "but you can be certain they understand and respect David. He's made great strides since coming here to Cutter Gap."

"But don't the souls in Richmond deserve saving just as much as the ones here?" Mrs. Grantland persisted.

"I believe the Lord's work can be done anywhere," Miss Alice said. Christy could hear the edge in her voice. It was the tone Miss Alice reserved for a wayward child.

"This is my calling, Mother," David said. "I belong here in Cutter Gap."

"Nonsense!" Mrs. Grantland cried. "You belong where you'll be properly appreciated."

"Isn't it really . . ." Christy paused. She felt strange, interrupting a conversation when she couldn't see the participants. "Isn't it David's choice, Mrs. Grantland? My parents weren't eager for me to come here, but in the end, they understood how important it was to me."

"Indeed. And look what happened to you."

Christy took a deep breath. "Still, I don't regret coming here. I've made so many friends—"

"I'm afraid," Mrs. Grantland interrupted, "that may be David's problem."

"And what problem is that, Mother?" David inquired.

"Oh, you know. Friends can keep you rooted to a place when it's time to move on." Christy had the strange feeling that Mrs. Grantland was looking right at her.

"Well," Miss Ida said after a moment of awkward silence, "I think it's time for me to clear the plates."

"I'll help," David said quickly.

"No, let me," said Miss Alice.

"Me, too," Ruby Mae chimed in.

"All of you stay put," Mrs. Grantland commanded. "There's something I must do. I've brought you all gifts."

"Presents!" Ruby Mae cried.

Christy could hear Mrs. Grantland swish across the dining room. She always seemed to move in great, flowing movements that made Christy think of an actress dashing across a stage.

"It was so hard to know what to bring," Mrs. Grantland said. "Now I see I could have brought everything but the kitchen sink. You *do* have a kitchen sink, don't you?"

"Yes, Mother," Miss Ida said, laughing.

"And a proper pump right outside," Ruby Mae added.

"Haven't you people heard of indoor plumbing?"

"We have, Mother," David replied. "But we think it's more fun tromping out into the yard in sub-zero temperatures to get a bucket of near-frozen water. It builds character."

"Don't you get sassy with your own mother," Mrs. Grantland chided, but it was clear she was laughing, too.

"This was very generous of you, Mother," David said.

"Oh, you know me. Any excuse to shop."

Christy heard the clasps of a trunk pop open, then the rustle of paper.

"I've brought plenty of books and magazines, of course," Mrs. Grantland began.

"Books!" Christy exclaimed. "That's wonderful! You have no idea how desperate the school is for reading material."

It occurred to her with a sudden pang that she might never again read another book. *No,* she told herself firmly. *No more thinking like that.*

"And I brought these for the mission house," Mrs. Grantland said.

Ruby Mae gasped. "Those gotta be the biggest diamonds in the world!"

"Actually, they're crystal, Ruby Mae," said Miss Alice. "Beautiful crystal candlesticks."

"They seem silly now," Mrs. Grantland said, for the first time sounding a little less sure of herself. "With all you need . . ."

"Quite the contrary," Miss Alice said gently. "They're a reminder of all the beauty in the world. A touch of magic. Thank you, Mrs. Grantland. It was very kind of you."

"And for Ida, a new dress. Goodness knows you need one."

"Oh, Mother! It's beautiful," Ida exclaimed.

"It's all shiny and blue with little stripes and bows and such," Ruby Mae whispered to Christy.

Mrs. Grantland placed a hand on Christy's shoulder. "And for you and Ruby Mae, I brought these lovely hats."

"For me?" Ruby Mae screeched. Christy felt the table jiggle as Ruby Mae leapt out of her chair. "You ain't havin' fun with me, are you, Mrs. Grantland?"

Mrs. Grantland laughed. "Of course not. Here. Try it on. And here's yours, Miss Huddleston."

"Please, call me Christy." Christy accepted the hat. She could feel the straw edges.

Around the brim were what felt like little silk roses.

"They're all a-covered with these pretend flowers, Miz Christy," Ruby Mae cried with excitement. "Sort of a pinkish color, like the sun when it's just comin' up." She paused. "Miz Grantland, I don't know if this would be rightly proper, considerin' that you're a preacher's mama and all, but would it be all right if I gave you a hug to say thank you kindly?"

"That's all right, dear—" Mrs. Grantland began, but David interrupted.

"Sure, Ruby Mae," he said. "Go on and give Mother a hug. Sort of an official welcome to Cutter Gap."

Christy heard footsteps, a rustle of skirts, then a slight *ugh* as Ruby Mae squeezed Mrs. Grantland.

"Miz Christy, ain't you goin' to try yours on?" Ruby Mae asked.

Carefully Christy placed the hat on her head. "I wish you could see how purty it looks!" Ruby Mae said.

Christy pulled off the hat and set it on the floor. "Thank you, Mrs. Grantland. That was very thoughtful of you."

"I hope it . . . I mean, if I'd known about your injury, perhaps I might have brought something more appropriate."

"Just because she's blind don't mean Miz

Christy can't wear purty things," Ruby Mae pointed out.

"Of course not," Mrs. Grantland said, her voice softening a little, "I only meant . . ." She paused, rummaging around in her trunk. "Anyway, last, but not least—for David, a new suit. From Whitman's in Richmond. Remember that tailor your father always used? I do hope you haven't lost so much weight you can't wear it."

"It's wonderful, Mother," David said. "Very impressive. And there are fine seamstresses here in the Cove who can alter it if need be. Thank you."

"It seems a little silly," Mrs. Grantland said with a sigh. "You could wear overalls to give your sermon and who would notice? That suit would be much better suited to a ministry back home."

David was silent. Miss Ida cleared her throat.

"Well, now that the gift-giving is over, I suppose we should get down to work, Christy," Miss Alice said at last. "That is, if you're feeling up to it. David and I want to go over your lesson plans. We're going to need to divide up the teaching work load. I expect we'll have to cut back quite a bit on school. Perhaps we'll shorten the school days so we can keep up with our other duties."

Christy let the words sink in. *Divide up the teaching work load.* Giving up her teaching duties felt like giving away part of herself. She felt a decision brewing, like a bubble in a pond slowly rising to the surface.

"You know, Mother was a teacher for many years," David said. Christy could almost *hear* the smile on his face. "Perhaps she wouldn't mind helping out a bit."

"David!" Mrs. Grantland objected. "I simply couldn't. I haven't set foot in a classroom in years. And those were *civilized* children—well-bred, with manners."

"What do you think about it, Christy?" David asked.

"In my experience," Christy said thoughtfully, "children are children, no matter where you go."

"I wouldn't hear of it," Mrs. Grantland said. "Sorry, David. You'll just have to recruit someone else. After all, you'll need to find a permanent replacement, anyway."

The room fell silent. The only sound was the clink of silverware as Ruby Mae finished her pie.

"I have an announcement to make," Christy said. Even as she slowly stood, she wasn't quite sure what she was going to say. But she felt something in her heart, urging her to speak.

"There won't be any need for a new teacher," Christy finally said. "Or for Miss Alice and David to divide up my teaching duties. I am going to continue teaching, as I always have. And I don't want any argument from anyone about this."

"Yahoo!" Ruby Mae cried.

"And there's one other thing," Christy added as the words rushed out. "David and I will be staying here in Cutter Gap permanently. As man and wife."

First, Christy heard gasps.

Then she heard a sigh.

Then she heard a very loud thud.

"What was that?" she asked.

"Miz Grantland," Ruby Mae replied. "She done took the news a little hard. She's plumb fainted straight away!"

❧ Nine ❧

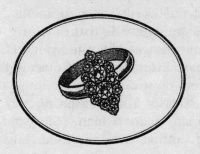

How's your mother?" Christy asked David a few minutes later.

"Miss Alice is tending to her on the couch. You'll have to forgive Mother. I told you she takes things *very* seriously." David sat down at the dining-room table with Christy. She could hear Ruby Mae and Miss Ida in the kitchen, talking in shocked whispers.

"Apparently I've caused quite a sensation," Christy said.

"You certainly have where I'm concerned. I'm not going to ask you why you made this decision," David said. "I'm only going to tell you how very glad you've made me."

"I'll tell you, anyway," Christy replied with a smile. "It was your sermon today. Listening to you, I realized that even if I have lost my sight forever, I can still be a teacher or a wife. I don't have to give up on my dreams. There are many ways to see. You're right about that. And now I'm going to prove it."

David fell silent for a moment. "So I'm a sort of experiment? Is that it?"

"No, no, not at all!" Christy cried. "It's just that today, listening to your beautiful words, I realized how deep my feelings really are for you, David. You're a strong and kind and gentle man, a good man." She smiled shyly. "And of course, you've got an awfully cute smile."

With trembling hands, David cupped Christy's face and gently kissed her.

"Oh. Oh, my. Excuse me—" It was Miss Ida, sounding very embarrassed.

"It's all right, Ida," David said. "Come on in. I am allowed to kiss my fiancée, aren't I?"

"Miss Ida," Christy said, "I'm so glad that we're going to practically be sisters."

"Welcome to the Grantland family," Miss Ida said stiffly, and then Christy heard her march off.

"Don't worry," David said. "She'll warm up to the idea."

"But she knows me," Christy said. "If Miss Ida's that set against it, how will I ever win over your mother?"

"With your incredible charm," David teased.

"Don't hold your breath," Christy said. "Why did you suggest she take my place teaching, anyway? Wasn't it obvious what she'd say?"

"Wishful thinking. I suppose I was hoping that if she got to know the students, she'd see why we love it here so."

"It's hard to imagine her having the patience to teach."

"Actually, she was quite good at it. But after my father died, she just sort of closed herself off. I know it's hard to believe, but she used to be much more . . . tolerant." David sighed. "I'd better go check on her. Want to come?"

"You think she can handle the strain?"

David took Christy's hand. They settled in the living room on two chairs across from the couch. "How are you feeling, Mother?" David asked.

"She'll be back to normal in no time," Miss Alice said.

"I'll be fine, with the grace of God," Mrs. Grantland said in a quavery voice. "No thanks to you two."

"I'm glad you're feeling better," Christy said.

"Miss Huddleston, my dear," said Mrs. Grantland. "Come here."

David helped Christy over to the couch, where Mrs. Grantland took her hand. "My dear girl, you must understand," she said. "I have nothing against you personally. I'm sure you're a fine girl. And I'm sure you'll go far in this world, even with your . . . your problem. But David is my only son. And I have such high hopes for him. Plans, great plans. He belongs in the right place, with the right people."

"You mean with Delia?" Christy asked with a smile.

Mrs. Grantland pulled away her hand. "As a matter of fact, I've always been very fond of Delia Manning. So refined and well-bred. And such a beauty! But that's not all I meant. I meant David doesn't belong here. Nor Ida. Nor you and Miss Alice, I'll wager. You're all decent folk. This is no place for your kind."

Someone knocked on the front door. "Come on in," David called. He lowered his voice. "We can only pray that it's decent folk."

The door flew open. Evening air, scented with spring flowers, cooled the room.

"Creed!" David exclaimed. "And Zach! What brings you two here?"

"We got some bad news, Preacher."

"Try to top what I just heard," Mrs. Grantland muttered.

"We done swum all afternoon over to the pond," Zach said. "Fished up the rowboat finally. It's right muddy but I 'spect it'll float again."

"I thought you said it was bad news," David said. "That's great."

"The bad news is we poked around every last inch o' that pond. We found two bullets, a belt buckle, and a moonshine jug. But there just ain't no sign o' that diamond ring anywheres."

"Diamond ring?" Mrs. Grantland repeated. "What diamond ring might that be? Who in this awful place owns a diamond ring?"

"The preacher did, ma'am," Creed answered. "He was sweetheartin' Miz Christy with it when he done dunked hisself and Miz Christy too and they—"

"Thank you for that very helpful information, Creed," David interrupted quickly. "Now, you boys need to be heading on home before it gets dark—"

"Sweetheartin'?" Mrs. Grantland repeated slowly. Christy felt her leap off the couch. "Great-great-grandmother Grantland's wedding ring? You *lost* her ring?"

"He didn't exactly lose it on purpose," Zach offered. "The way I hear tell, it was Miz Christy who was a-holdin' it—"

"You! YOU lost it?"

"Well, it was an accident, really—" Christy began, but she was interrupted by another loud thud.

The room went still.

"It seems," David informed Christy, "that Mother's fainted yet again."

"Is she dead?" Creed whispered.

"No, Creed," Christy replied with a sigh. "Just dead set against me."

"You think I'm completely crazy, don't you?" Christy asked Miss Alice the next morning as they walked up the steps to the school. Christy wanted to get there well before the students started arriving.

"What are you referring to?" Miss Alice said as she held open the door. "Your return to the classroom? Or your engagement to David?"

"Either. Both," Christy said, laughing.

They stepped inside. Instantly Christy felt the warm reassuring feeling she always had when she was here. *This is where you belong*, the room seemed to say. *This is home*.

Christy let go of Miss Alice's arm and began making her way toward her desk. In her mind she tried to picture the arrangement of desks and benches. The blackboard would be just over to the right. Zach's desk was just a foot or two away, and over there was the bench where Ruby Mae and Bessie Coburn and Lizette Holcombe always sat.

Slowly she navigated her way through the maze of obstacles. "See how easy it is?" she asked. "I know this room like the back of my hand."

"You do indeed. But I think you're going to have to realize something, Christy. It's not a sin to ask for help."

"I don't need any help," Christy said firmly.

She bumped into a long desk and realized she'd reached her destination. Lovingly she ran her fingers over the rough wood, with its carved initials and gouges.

"Everyone needs help sometimes."

Christy put her hands on her hips. "You're the one who said I could teach again."

"And I still think so. But I think you're going to have to do it differently."

"I am going to be the same teacher I always was, Miss Alice." Christy settled into her chair. "Any less would be cheating the children."

Miss Alice was quiet for a moment. "Well, I am here, if you need me. We all are."

"Thank you," Christy said. "Really."

"Are you sure you don't want someone to stay with you today? I've got a patient to tend to, but perhaps—"

"No. I want to do this myself. All by myself."

Christy heard Miss Alice walk toward the door. Suddenly she felt very alone. "Miss Alice?" she called. "What do you think about David and me getting married?"

"I think," Miss Alice said gently, "that only you can know what's in your heart, Christy. But when we make a commitment, a big commitment, it's important to be sure we're doing it for the right reasons."

The right reasons? What does she mean by that? Christy wondered.

"Why, hello there, Neil," Miss Alice said suddenly.

Christy heard the sound of boots on the wooden steps.

"You're making a mistake, Christy," the doctor said darkly.

"Word certainly travels fast in these parts," Miss Alice commented. "I'll leave you two to talk."

"A mistake?" Christy repeated as the doctor approached her desk. "You mean about teaching?"

"About teaching and a whole lot more," the doctor barked. "You're trying to prove that nothing's changed. And you're making a mistake that could ruin the rest of your life."

"I'm ready to teach, Neil. I have to teach."

"Maybe. Maybe not. But you're not ready to marry. At least . . . at least not him."

Christy tapped a pencil against the desk, trying to control her anger. "Who are you to tell me what I'm ready to do? Who are you to tell me whom I should marry?"

The doctor grabbed her by the shoulders. "I know you, Christy," he said, with such intensity she could practically see the pain in his eyes. "I know you want to prove you can take on the world. But this is not the way to do it."

"Why does everyone doubt me?" Christy cried. "Miss Alice just got done telling me I can't teach without help. Now here you are, marching up to tell me that I can't marry David because you think I don't love him."

"I didn't say that," the doctor pointed out. "You did."

"Of *course* I love him. I feel safe with David. And I admire him. And I know he loves me."

"And me?" the doctor asked softly. "What about me?"

"Neil, you make me feel happy, and I like talking to you. But you can also make me angrier than anyone I know. David is predictable. But you, Neil, just make me feel . . . too many things at once. And at the moment you're making me very angry."

The doctor took a step backwards. "I hope you'll be very happy," he snapped.

"You're invited to the wedding, of course," Christy said, trying to sound happier than she felt.

The doctor gave a harsh laugh. "I plan to be busy that day," he said, and with that, he was gone.

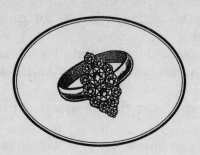

Ten

When the doctor had left, the only sound was the soft whoosh of the pine trees swaying outside the window. Christy stood, trying to rein in her anger.

She could picture the schoolhouse perfectly in her mind. To her right sat the girls; to her left, the boys. She imagined the first row of girls. Ruby Mae, Bessie, Lizette, Clara. Or was it Clara, then Lizette? They changed places so often, it was hard to know.

Carefully Christy paced off the distance to the blackboard. One, two, three, four, five. Five steps, and if she reached out her arm, there was the board. Would she be able to write on the board legibly? Yes, if she really concentrated. She'd always had excellent penmanship. She'd just have to imagine the letters, one by one.

You're making a mistake. She heard the doctor's voice in her head as if he were still there in the room. Never had he sounded so angry. Well, he had no right to tell her what to do. This was her life, after all.

"There she is!"

"David?" Christy turned toward the voice. "Is that you?"

"I've brought you a visitor."

Christy caught a whiff of the rose perfume. "Mrs. Grantland! What a . . . surprise."

"How did you—"

"Your perfume." Christy took five careful steps back to her desk. She bumped her chair with her knee, then sat down. "David, I really don't think today is a good day for visitors . . ."

David perched on her desk. "I was going to stay and help you myself," he said, lowering his voice to a whisper, "but Ida just informed me that the pump's not working, and unless I fix it, we're going to be mighty thirsty come evening. I thought Mother could stick around and help you out, just in case things get hectic."

"David!" Christy said. "I just don't—"

"I want you two to get to know each other," David insisted under his breath. "If she knows you better, she'll understand why I love you so much. Besides, I'll feel a lot better knowing there's someone here in case you need help."

"I want to do this myself, David." Christy sighed deeply.

"I know. She'll stay out of your way, I promise."

"If she annoys me, I'm going to ask her to leave."

"Fair enough." David took her hand. "Are you sure you're up to this?"

"Absolutely."

"All right, then. Oh. I almost forgot." Christy felt him slip something onto the ring finger of her left hand.

"What's this?"

"A makeshift engagement ring. It's just a piece of red ribbon from Ida's sewing box. The best I could do on short notice."

"It'll do very nicely till we find the ring."

David kissed her cheek. "*If* we find it. Now, if you need anything, you just yell, all right? And don't hesitate to ask Mother for help. She was a teacher, after all."

When David left, the room was silent. If it hadn't been for the perfume, Christy would have been sure his mother had left with him.

"Mrs. Grantland?"

"Yes. I'm still here."

"I know David meant well, asking you to stay. But I really don't need any help. I intend to do this myself."

"Young lady, I don't want to be here any more than you want me. But my son insists that you two are going through with this betrothal. Moreover, he insists I spend time with you. And since I do not know anything about repairing pumps, and since my daughter is busy tending to chickens, of all the disgusting things, this is the only recreation left to me. You would think after I came all the way from Richmond, my children would at least have the decency to entertain their poor mother."

"Well, you're welcome to take a seat and observe," Christy said coolly. She had enough to worry about without taking care of David's mother. She knew he meant well, but having an audience was just going to make Christy *more* nervous.

"Miz Christy! You really *are* here!"

Christy recognized the voice instantly as Lulu Spencer's, a sweet six-year-old who was one of Fairlight's daughters. An instant later, Lulu was in Christy's lap, offering her a warm hug. "I was afeared you weren't comin', on account of your eyes not working."

"I'm here, all right," Christy said. "I can still teach even if my eyes aren't working, don't you think?"

Lulu thought for a moment. "I reckon so."

Within minutes, the schoolroom was buzzing with children. Each one came over to greet Christy. They seemed fascinated by her bandages. Christy tried to keep a mental count of the students as they arrived, but she lost count after thirty.

Although she couldn't see, it amazed her

what she could hear. It was as if her ears were working harder, to compensate for her lack of sight. She heard marbles on the floor in the southeast corner. She heard sniffles coming from the second row on the boys' side. Was that Little Burl Allen, with yet another cold? She heard whispers coming from the back of the room—no doubt Lundy Taylor and Smith O'Teale, the class bullies. She heard an argument brewing in the back of the room—two of the younger children, fighting over a rag doll. She heard two other children playing tic-tac-toe on the blackboard.

It was so much information! She didn't know what to do with it all. With her eyes, she could make sense of the classroom. She could tell where a real fight was starting, and when it was just a silly squabble she could ignore. She could tell who had dark circles under their eyes from staying up late doing chores, and who was gaunt from hunger. Those were students who wouldn't be able to concentrate, and she would know to take it easy on them.

But she couldn't know any of those things. Not anymore.

The noise in the room swelled. A paper airplane hit her in the shoulder. The children knew that was against the rules, since they couldn't afford to waste a single piece of paper. She felt a wave of panic. This was insane! She couldn't handle all these children! No one could!

Calm down, she told herself. Hadn't she thought exactly the same thing on her first day of teaching? Her knees had been shaking so hard that even the children had noticed.

"All right, children," Christy said in her best stern-teacher voice. "Settle down." She gripped the edge of the desk for support. "I want you all to take your seats."

She heard the shuffle of bare feet on the wooden floor. Shouts turned to whispers.

All right, that was a good sign. At least they were still willing to obey her.

"Now, today is a special day for two reasons," Christy began. "First of all, we have a visitor. The Reverend Grantland's mother is here, all the way from Richmond, Virginia. So I want you to all be on your best behavior."

"She smells like roses, Teacher," Creed said.

"Yes, Creed. That's called perfume. It's made from flowers."

"Well, do I got to sit next to her all day? It's like sittin' next to a rosebush in full bloom. My nose will like to burst!"

"Creed, that is very rude," Christy chided. "Don't you think you should apologize to Mrs. Grantland?"

"Gee whiz, Miz Grantland, I didn't mean no offense—"

"Apology accepted. Perhaps, Miss Huddleston, if you taught these children some basic hygiene skills, they wouldn't object to the scent of perfume."

"Thank you for the advice, Mrs. Grantland." Christy turned to the left, where the map of the United States was tacked to the wall.

"I wonder if someone can find Richmond on a map of the United States?" she asked.

"Me, Teacher!"

"Pick me, Teacher!"

"I knows it for sure!"

When the children all spoke at once, it was very hard to tell their voices apart. And although she'd taught them to raise their hands, that wouldn't help her now.

"Sam Houston? Did you want to point out Richmond?"

"No'm. I ain't got my hand a-raised. Try Wraight."

"Wraight?"

"He knows I ain't got my hand up no ways," Wraight cried. "Sam Houston Holcombe, I'm a-goin' to whop you good at recess for that!"

"Boys, that's quite enough," Christy said sternly. If she wasn't careful, she was going to lose control of the class. "John Spencer, why don't you show all of us where Richmond is located?"

John, one of her best students, was a safe choice. She heard him walk over to the map. Suddenly she realized there was no way to know whether he was correct. It was likely, since he was a good student. But how could she be sure?

The questions multiplied in her head. How was she going to grade papers? How was she going to write up tests?

How was she going to discipline students at recess? How was she going to bandage a scraped knee?

How was she going to know if John had just pointed out Richmond or not?

Panic surged through her like lightening. In her heart, she'd known these problems were waiting for her. She just hadn't wanted to admit it. *This is crazy,* a voice in her head cried. *You can't do this. Not in a million years.*

"I . . . I, uh . . ." Christy stammered.

"Correct," came a shrill voice from the back of the room. "What was your name again? John?"

"Yes'm, Mrs. Grantland."

Christy sighed with relief. She'd gotten through that minor crisis, but not without some unwelcome assistance.

"Very good, John," she said. "You may go back to your seat."

"Miz Christy?"

"Yes? Is that Creed?"

"You done said there were two reasons this day was special."

"So I did. The other reason is that this is the start of an experiment. An experiment is a sort of test, to see if something is true or false. And what I am trying to find out is whether or not I can teach without my sight. I think I can—at least, I *hope* I can. So you see, in a way, you are part of the experiment."

"Miz Christy?"

"Yes, Creed."

"We done brought you something for the 'speriment."

A moment later, Christy felt something pressed into her hands.

"It's a cane," Creed explained. "Zach and Sam Houston and I made it outa oak."

"Like my granny's!" Mountie exclaimed.

Christy felt the carefully smoothed wood. "Boys, I can tell it's beautiful. Thank you very much. I needed one. And I will be proud to use it."

In truth, Christy had talked herself into believing she could get by without a cane. But she had to admit that was silly. Even if she memorized every square foot of the mission property, how was she going to navigate through the yard when it rained or snowed, unless she had a cane?

"Miz Christy?"

"Who was that?"

"Me, Lizette. Is it true about you and the preacher gettin' hitched?"

Mrs. Grantland let out a loud sigh.

"Yes," Christy said, "it is true. And you're all invited to the wedding."

Mrs. Grantland let out a much louder sigh.

"Miz Christy?"

"Yes, Creed?"

"Is there somethin' wrong with the preacher's mama? She's breathin' awful funny."

"There's nothing wrong with me that a little dose of reality couldn't cure," Mrs. Grantland muttered.

Christy cleared her throat. *Penmanship*, she told herself. *That's a good idea. Don't think about all the things that could go wrong. Don't think about the doctor yelling. Or David's mother sighing. Or the fact that Lundy Taylor is undoubtedly tossing spitballs from the back of the room by now.*

"I think we'll start today by working on our penmanship," Christy said. Carefully she headed to the blackboard. One, two, three, four—

With a thud, she hit the board, nose-first. The pain was horrible. The board teetered back and forth on its wobbly wooden legs.

"Look out!" someone yelled.

Christy tried to grab it, but it was too late. The board went crashing to the ground. Slate shattered into pieces that skittered across the floor.

The children were silent. Even Mrs. Grantland kept quiet.

"Miz Christy?" Creed whispered.

Christy rubbed her head. "Yes, Creed?"

"Does this mean the 'speriment's over?"

"No, Creed," Christy said wearily. "It just means it's going to be a *very* long experiment."

❧ Eleven ❧

It was awful," Christy said at dinner that evening. "Just awful. I broke the blackboard. I tripped over the water bucket. I stepped on one of the hogs at recess. I gave a math quiz and couldn't grade it." She shook her head. "I looked ridiculous."

"To whom?" Miss Alice asked gently. "To the children? Or to yourself?"

Christy shrugged. "Both, I guess."

"You didn't look foolish to none of us, Miz Christy," Ruby Mae said. As usual, her mouth was full of food. "I mean, a couple kids snickered some when you sat on your sandwich at lunchtime. Mostly Lundy and them older boys. But it weren't so bad."

Mrs. Grantland let out a long sigh. Christy had heard that sigh so many times today, she knew it like her own voice. Still, she had to admit that Mrs. Grantland *had* come to her rescue several times—not that Christy had wanted her to.

"Personally, I think it's insane for you to try to teach—sight or no sight," Mrs. Grantland said. "That's the most awful excuse for a schoolroom I've ever seen! And the filthy children! No shoes, no clean clothes, no manners, no proper English, no respect for authority . . ."

"I ain't dirty," Ruby Mae said proudly. "I wash behind my ears and everything. Wanna see?"

"I'll take your word for it, dear."

"Are all city folks as prissy as you, Miz Grantland?" Ruby Mae asked.

"Prissy?"

"You shoulda seen her, Preacher," Ruby Mae said. "Creed done brought a black snake to school. When he handed it to your mama, she musta jumped halfway to heaven."

David laughed loudly.

"David!" Mrs. Grantland scolded.

"Sorry, Mother," David said. "It's just that I was remembering that time when Ida and I brought home a toad. I couldn't have been more than eight. We named him Harold, remember, Ida?"

"Mother was none too happy about Harold," Ida recalled.

Mrs. Grantland even laughed a little. "Well,

you were generally very well-behaved children. That was just . . . the exception that proves the rule. But these children are another story altogether."

"I'm very sorry about the snake, Mrs. Grantland," Christy said. "If I'd known . . ."

"No matter," Mrs. Grantland said. "It's just an example of why you're taking on more than any person could possibly handle. When I was a teacher, the children knew their place. No talking back, no—what are they called?—salivaballs—"

"Spitballs, ma'am," Ruby Mae interrupted politely.

"—and certainly no snakes. And the sheer number! Sixty-seven students, of all ages and abilities. Why, that's enough for three classrooms. It's madness."

"Suppose we all take shifts, Christy?" David asked. "Ida and Miss Alice and I—and maybe Mother, too, while she's here? We could act as assistants, like Mother did today. Just help out till you get things under control."

"I can't ask you to do that," Christy said. "You've all got your own work to do. And I'll wager your mother has seen all she needs of my classroom."

"Goodness me, yes!" Mrs. Grantland exclaimed.

"If I'm going to do this," Christy vowed, "I'm going to do this myself."

Mrs. Grantland leaned across the table and touched Christy's hand. "I'm just telling you the truth, my dear. It's impossible. You simply can't handle that group of hooligans all by yourself."

"What's a hooligan, Miz Christy?" Ruby Mae asked.

"It's what you'll be if you don't help me clear these dishes," Miss Ida said sternly. Then under her breath she explained, "It's a troublemaker."

Christy leaned back in her chair while Ruby Mae cleared away her plate. "What do you think, Miss Alice?" she asked. "Is Mrs. Grantland right?"

"I believe she's right that you have set before you a very large task," Miss Alice said, choosing her words in that slow, careful way she had. "But I also believe you can handle it, *if* you recognize your limitations. As I said, it's no sin to ask for help, Christy."

The Lord does not give us more than we can handle.

Christy thought of the words she'd scribbled in her diary the night of her accident. No, she was not going to ask for help. She was going to prove that she was everything she ever was. She was going to do this alone.

Otherwise, it would mean admitting what she'd lost.

"No, thank you, Miss Alice," Christy said

firmly. "I have to try to do this by myself. You can understand that, can't you?"

Miss Alice didn't answer right away. "I came across a book among the many Mrs. Grantland brought us. It's called *The Story of My Life*, by a woman named Helen Keller."

"I remember reading something about her in the newspaper back home in Asheville," Christy said.

"She was left blind and deaf after an illness," Miss Alice explained. "But with the help of a gifted teacher named Anne Sullivan, she was able to learn to communicate. Now she travels the country, giving speeches and raising money on behalf of the handicapped."

"So you're saying if she can accomplish that, so can I?" Christy asked.

"Yes, I'm saying that. And I'm also saying she didn't get where she is today without the help of others."

With a sigh, Christy reached for her new cane and pushed back her chair. "If you'll excuse me," she said, "I'll be heading off to bed. I've got a busy day planned for tomorrow. We're having a spelling bee."

"I'll say one thing for that girl," Christy heard Mrs. Grantland comment as she walked away, "she's certainly as stubborn as they come!"

By Friday, Christy felt like the week had held a hundred days in it. She was exhausted and bruised. Her morale was shaken. She'd broken, bumped, or tripped over more things than she'd ever imagined possible. She'd never realized how full of obstacles the world was.

As she sat on the schoolhouse steps at recess, she tried to tell herself that things were improving. That she was getting the hang of being a blind teacher to sixty-seven difficult students. That she was just as good a teacher as she'd ever been.

But she knew it wasn't true.

This morning, when she'd sat down at her chair, she'd known it all over again. She'd heard the delicate crack of an egg, then felt the gooey insides soaking her skirt.

It was a harmless prank, no doubt Lundy Taylor's doing, but it was the kind of thing that never would have happened in the old days.

Worse than that sort of embarrassment was the feeling she couldn't reach her children as well. Without being able to see their beautiful faces, she couldn't know all the stories hidden there. Pain, hunger, and sometimes joy—their eyes revealed it all. But she couldn't see them anymore.

"I'll git you for that, you slimy little tree toad!"

Christy heard a shout, then a scream, then the sound of scuffling in the schoolyard. She grabbed her cane.

"Teacher! Teacher! Come quick! Lundy's a-beatin' on Creed somethin' fierce!"

Christy started toward the noise of the fight, but her skirt caught on a shrub and she tripped.

"Awwoww!" came a boy's scream. "Stop it, Lundy! I give, I give!"

"Lundy!" Christy cried as she struggled to her feet. "Lundy Taylor! You stop that this instant!"

"And what're you goin' to do, blind lady?" The voice was coming from her right, about twenty feet away. "Whop me with your cane?"

Christy heard the terrible sound of a fist meeting flesh. Creed howled with pain.

Frantically, Christy ran toward the crying boy. She hit a solid wall that turned out to be Lundy. She grabbed him by the shoulders and shook him with all her might, even though he stood several inches taller and weighed far more than she did.

"You ain't a-goin' to hurt me," he sneered. "You're blind as a bat!" He took a step backward and she lost her grip on him. "What're you goin' to do now? Whop me with your cane? I can beat up on this whole school and there ain't no way you're a-goin' to stop me."

Nearby, Creed was sobbing on the ground.

Christy heard what sounded like a sharp kick, and Creed cried out again.

"Lundy!" Christy screamed. "Stop it, now!"

"You don't scare me none," Lundy said.

The sense of helplessness was more than she could bear. Filled with rage, Christy lifted the cane high into the air, ready to strike.

Then she heard a shout. "No! Don't do it!"

❧ Twelve ❧

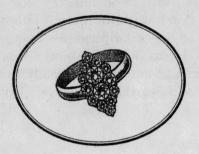

Please, Miss Huddleston, stop!"

It was Mrs. Grantland. There was a busy rustling of skirts, and a moment later, the scent of roses filled the air.

"What on earth is going on here, young man?" Mrs. Grantland demanded. "Lundy, isn't that your name?"

"Teacher's a-beatin' on me with her cane," Lundy whimpered in a pathetic voice. "You seen it."

"I'll wager you did something quite abominable to warrant your teacher's wrath," Mrs. Grantland said. "Not that I'd blame her one whit for taking a switch to you."

Christy lowered her arm. She felt horrified at her own actions and humiliated that Mrs. Grantland had seen her.

"Mrs. Grantland, I can handle this," she said shakily.

But Mrs. Grantland wasn't listening. "Lundy, did you hit this little boy?" she demanded.

"He had it comin'—" Lundy began.

"I want you to apologize to him this instant," said Mrs. Grantland.

"You ain't my teacher. And I ain't sayin' sorry to someone who's lower than a snake belly in a wagon rut—"

"Apologize," Mrs. Grantland commanded. "Now."

Christy could hear Lundy's breathing. She could hear Creed's sobs. Then, to her amazement, she heard Lundy mutter, "Get up, you twit-wit. I'm sorry, I reckon."

Mrs. Grantland clapped her hands firmly. "The rest of you, back into the classroom. And I do not mean maybe."

Christy listened to the whispers as the children filed sullenly back into class. "Creed?" she called. "Are you all right?"

The little boy ran up to her. "Right as rain, Miz Christy. I'll have a mighty fine bruise, though. Ain't bad. Lundy's done beat me up much worse." With that, he ran off whistling, as if nothing were wrong.

But something was very wrong. Suddenly, the enormity of what had happened hit Christy.

It was bad enough that Mrs. Grantland, of all people, had stepped in to control Lundy. It was far worse that Christy had raised her hand in anger at one of the children—even if it *was* Lundy Taylor, a vicious bully.

Worst of all was the fact that she hadn't been able to protect one of the children. Creed had been in danger, because of her.

"There now," Mrs. Grantland said briskly. "All settled. Everyone's back inside. That Lundy creature is a torment, isn't he? How you handle him is beyond me."

"I couldn't handle him, obviously. You did."

"Oh, he was just startled by the sound of my disciplinarian voice." Mrs. Grantland laughed. "Haven't used that in many years. I have to admit, I rather enjoyed it."

"What were you doing here, anyway? Did David send you to check up on me again?"

"No, I was just going for a walk. These mountains are rather interesting. Richmond's so flat by comparison." She hesitated. "If the truth be told, I've walked past the school every day this week, right around this time."

"Spying on me," Christy said bitterly.

"Not exactly. I just . . ." Mrs. Grantland's voice trailed off. "I suppose I was intrigued."

"Intrigued by what?"

"By how you were managing. It's not that I *care*, one way or the other," she added stiffly. "It's just that, as a former teacher, I kept wondering how it was possible you could pull it off. Professional curiosity, you might call it."

"And now you have your answer," Christy snapped. "I can't! I was fooling myself, thinking I could do this. You knew and David knew and Doctor MacNeill knew. But no, I had to be The Great Christy, capable of magically pulling off the impossible." Her throat tightened. "My own vanity put these children at risk. I've been dealing with Lundy for months, and I've never been that out of control. What if I had hit him? What if he had really hurt Creed?"

Mrs. Grantland did not say anything.

"You know I'm right," Christy said.

"The truth is, dear, I don't think anyone could do what you tried to do. If you must know, I'm not particularly pleased at being right."

"Of course you're pleased," Christy cried. "You don't want me to marry David. If I can't stay here and teach, then you think he'll return to Richmond with you."

"I have hopes, certainly . . . but I'm starting to think it's not quite that simple," Mrs. Grantland said softly. "He seems to really care about these people."

"Well, if you won't say it, I will. I shouldn't be a teacher. I can't be a teacher."

"I know we aren't exactly allies, Miss Huddleston. But whatever my feelings about your engagement to David, I'm very sorry about what's happened to you."

Christy tossed her cane across the yard in disgust. She winced when she heard the sharp crack as it hit a tree.

"Tell them class is dismissed," she told Mrs. Grantland. "I'm sure you'll enjoy that duty."

"I was totally out of control," Christy confessed the next day as Doctor MacNeill checked her bandages. "I've never been so angry."

Why was she confiding in the doctor? When he'd checked on her throughout the week, they'd barely spoken. She knew he was still angry about her engagement to David. Still, he somehow seemed like the only person who would understand her anger.

"It's natural," the doctor said. "You're upset about what's happened to you. You've been holding it all inside. It was bound to come out, sooner or later."

"But I was so rude to Mrs. Grantland. I apologized this morning and she told me she understood, but I don't see how she could have. I wanted to lash out at someone, and she seemed like the perfect target. I was just mad because she was right about my trying to teach."

"Come on," the doctor said suddenly.

"What?"

"We're going for a walk, you and I. Fresh air will do you good. Doctor's orders."

"I thought . . . I thought you were mad at me. About the engagement."

"I am," the doctor said flatly. "But you need a friend today. And it looks like I'm elected."

Christy took the doctor's arm as they walked

through the woods. The birds were in full chorus. The sun teased her shoulders. The smell of pine was as refreshing as a splash of icy water on her face.

"I've noticed one thing about not having my sight," Christy said. "I do 'see' things differently. The sounds, the smells—they're so much more intense. It's as if I'm experiencing the world in a whole new way."

"I suppose you are."

"Neil?"

"Hmm?"

"When can we take the bandages off?"

He stopped. "Another week, perhaps. When the swelling is down a bit more."

"I almost took them off last night," Christy admitted. "I just wanted to know for sure. To be done with it."

"You need more time."

The doctor resumed walking, and Christy fell into step beside him. "I wish . . ." he began. "I wish there were something more I could do about your eyes. I feel so inadequate."

The anguish in his voice made her heart ache. "This is in God's hands, Neil. There's nothing more you can do."

"There are other ways I feel inadequate," the doctor continued. His voice was so soft she could barely hear it over the chattering of the birds. "I wish . . . I wish I could tell you—"

"Tell me what?"

"Remember that night? That night when

Ruby Mae was lost and you went out to find her in the storm? I was so worried about you! And then when you came back safely, and we sat by the fire, and we . . . we danced together . . ."

"I remember," Christy said softly. "You danced very well even with one arm in a sling."

"I guess it *was* a bit awkward." The doctor gave a rueful laugh. "But I just want you to know, Christy—that night will always be with me."

"Me, too," Christy said softly.

"If you aren't going to teach anymore, does that mean you're leaving Cutter Gap?"

"I don't know," Christy said. "I suppose that depends on what David wants to do."

At the mention of David's name, Christy felt the doctor stiffen. "You need to learn to listen to your own heart, Christy Huddleston," he said. "I love the stubbornness in you, but sometimes it just plain gets in the way of your hearing what you need to hear."

They walked in silence after that. Christy listened to the crackle of sticks beneath their feet, and the flutter of wings overhead. But mostly she listened as the doctor softly hummed an old Scottish folk song about lost love.

Somehow, the sweet, sad tune seemed to be coming from her very own heart.

❧ Thirteen ❧

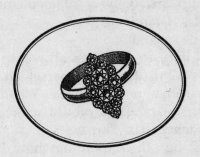

On Monday morning, Christy did not bother getting dressed. She stood at the open window of her bedroom in her robe and listened to the shouts and laughter of her students floating on the breeze. Miss Alice and David were taking over her teaching duties until another teacher could be found.

It had all been decided at dinner last night. David felt it was for the best. Miss Alice had not expressed an opinion. Neither, for that matter, had Mrs. Grantland—much to Christy's surprise.

The knock on her door startled her. "Christy?"

"Miss Alice! Come in. I thought you were teaching this morning."

"I've been called away. It seems Ben Pentland broke his ankle last night, and

Neil's busy over at the Holcombes with their sick baby. David's in El Pano this morning, picking up that delivery of medicine, which leaves Mrs. Grantland."

"Mrs. Grantland!"

"She'll have to do. She's all we've got."

"But—" Christy stopped herself. It was not her classroom, not anymore. Whatever her faults, Mrs. Grantland would make a much better teacher than Christy.

"I must be off. Is there anything I can get you before I go?" Miss Alice asked.

"Nothing. I'm fine. Be careful," Christy said.

She returned to the window. The bell in the steeple was ringing. The children would be running to their desks. Creed, of course, would be showing up late, no doubt with some new wild animal in tow. Ruby Mae would be giggling with Bessie about their latest crushes. John Spencer would have his head buried in the book of poetry Christy had lent him.

Would Mrs. Grantland know to be gentle with Mountie? She embarrassed so easily. Would she know that Zach had trouble with his eyesight? Would she . . .

Stop it, Christy told herself. They weren't her students anymore. She was not their teacher anymore. And it was a good thing, too.

She climbed back into bed. For a change,

she could sleep in. She could sleep in every morning, from now on.

She closed her eyes. The laughter of the children traveled on the breeze like the chatter of birds. Try as she might, she could not seem to sleep.

— — —

It wasn't until afternoon that Christy finally bothered to get dressed. Miss Ida had already stopped by twice to make sure she was all right.

Christy was just lacing up her shoes when she heard a shy knock on the door. "I'm all right, Miss Ida," Christy said. "I'm actually getting dressed, you'll be pleased to hear."

"Teacher! It's me, Creed!"

"Creed!" Christy rushed to the door, fumbling for the knob. "Is something wrong at school?"

"You just gotta come quick-like, Teacher! It's plumb awful! Lundy Taylor's done tied up Miz Grantland to her chair. And Sam Houston let the hogs loose in the schoolroom. And Ruby Mae and them girls are havin' a square dance, a-singin' and carryin' on. I swear it's true! It's like the whole school's gone plumb crazy!"

Christy hesitated. What could she do? Maybe she should send Miss Ida instead. After last

Friday, Christy knew better than to presume she could handle things alone. Still, if Mrs. Grantland really *was* tied up, that called for quick action.

Christy allowed Creed to lead her by the hand across the yard to the schoolhouse. Strangely, as they got closer, she couldn't hear any noise coming from the school. As a matter of fact, the place was eerily quiet.

"I thought you said they were having a square dance."

"Yes'm, they is." Creed hesitated. "I mean, they was, and if they isn't, well, it's probably 'cause that Lundy's done somethin' powerful mean."

"Creed." Christy stopped and knelt down. "There's something I need to say to you. I am very, very sorry that I broke the cane you made me. Sometimes even adults get angry and have temper tantrums. I felt angry at myself because I wasn't able to protect you from Lundy. And I'm very sorry that I broke that beautiful cane. Can you forgive me?"

"Shucks, Teacher. It weren't nothin'. I have powerful good tantrums my own self."

Christy laughed.

"Besides, we already made—"

"What?"

"Nothin'. Come on." He tugged on her arm. "Miz Grantland's gotta be goin' plumb crazy by now."

Slowly, Christy ascended the wooden schoolhouse steps with Creed's help. She thought she heard vague whisperings, but that was all.

"Mrs. Grantland?" Christy called from the doorway. "Is everything all right?"

Suddenly the entire room burst into song:

For she's a jolly good teacher,
For she's a jolly good teacher,
For she's a jolly good teacher,
Which nobody can deny!

Christy gasped. "What in the world?"

"Sorry, Teacher," Creed said. "I kinda told a fib to get you here. Well, a bunch o' fibs. See, it's a 'speriment."

"I don't understand."

"You will, soon enough." It was Mrs. Grantland's voice.

"Mrs. Grantland? Are you . . . are you by any chance tied to a chair?"

"Goodness, no. Although if I gave these hooligans half a chance, no doubt they'd try it. Creed, take Miss Christy to her seat."

She started toward her desk, but Christy felt a tug on her arm. "Follow me, Teacher. We done made some changes."

Christy followed Creed to her desk. No longer was it located on the raised platform she'd tripped on so often last week. Now it was on the lower level, where the students' desks were.

She sat down obediently. "Mrs. Grantland," she began, "this is all very nice, but I really don't—"

"John Spencer, why don't you begin?" Mrs. Grantland interrupted.

Christy heard John clear his throat. "We got together and sort of come to the conclusion that we wasn't helpin' any with your experiment, Miz Christy," he said. "We put together some ideas we kinda wanted to run by you. To start with, we got ourselves some—what was they called, Miz Grantland?"

"Monitors."

"Yeah. We got us some monitors. First off is Ruby Mae Morrison. She's the noise monitor, on account of she's usually the one making it."

Everyone laughed.

"My job is to get the class to hush, Miz Christy," Ruby Mae announced. "And I aim to do it, too!"

"Next off is Sam Houston," John said. "He's the hand monitor."

"Hand monitor?" Christy repeated.

"I tell you who-all's waving their hands, Teacher. And if you want, I can pick who answers, too. Like as not, I can tell who's done homework and who's just a-fakin' it."

"Lizette is board monitor," John continued,

"on account of she's got the best handwriting. 'Ceptin' for you, Miz Christy. And I'm map monitor. On account of I know where all the states is."

Christy began to smile, in spite of herself.

"Me! Don't forget me!" came a loud, boy's voice.

Christy recognized it as Wraight Holt's. "What's your job, Wraight?" she asked.

"I'm the recess monitor," Wraight explained. "Which is most likely the most important monitorin' goin' on. I round up all the little ones when you says it's time. *And* I break up all the fights."

"'Less'n he started 'em," Lundy Taylor said.

"Actually," Mrs. Grantland broke in, "I think Mountie O'Teale has the most important job."

"And what might that be?" Christy asked.

"I'm the bell monitor," Mountie proclaimed in her gentle voice. "If'n Lundy does some bullyin' or we all get too hard to handle, I get to pull the church bell so the preacher or Miss Alice can come a-runnin'."

"What about me?" tiny five-year-old Vella Holt demanded.

"What is it you're monitoring, Vella?" Christy asked.

"I'm the chair monitor!" Vella exclaimed proudly. "I check it for eggs or tacks or anything else that might be a-lurkin'."

"There's more, too," Mrs. Grantland continued. "We've done some rearranging to make things easier. Your desk is off the platform, for one thing. And the desks are arranged so that all the children are in a semi-circle. I thought it might be easier for you to address them that way. The children are seated alphabetically, too."

"Boys and girls together?" Christy cried. She hadn't yet been able to convince the children to stop dividing up, with boys on one side and girls on the other.

"It's a mighty big favor to be askin'," Creed said, "seein' as I'm stuck next to Wanda Beck. But we did it for you, Teacher."

"Creed!" Sam Houston urged. "The present!"

"I almost forgot!"

Christy felt something placed in her lap. Instantly she knew. It was a new cane, even smoother and larger than the last one.

"It's beautiful, children," Christy whispered. "I don't know what to say."

All this planning, for her! It was so thoughtful, and she knew the children meant well. But what kind of teacher would she be, relying on her own students for such help?

"Was this your doing, Mrs. Grantland?" Christy asked.

"Quite the contrary. The children came up with the idea last Friday after you left. I just added some pointers."

"The thing is, Miz Christy," John said, "we want to help make the experiment work. I mean, seein' as we're a part of it and all, it only seems right."

They *were* a part of it, Christy realized. She'd been so busy thinking about her own need to prove herself, she hadn't thought about *their* need to be involved.

"I've never seen such goings-on for a teacher," Mrs. Grantland said. "All I ever got was an apple or two. Of course . . . maybe I didn't give as much, either."

"I don't know what to say," Christy admitted.

"Say you'll do the 'speriment, Teacher," Creed pleaded.

Christy took a deep breath. This wasn't how she'd wanted it to be. But then, maybe it was even better, in a way.

"Get out your history books," she announced, and the whole class cheered.

⚜ Fourteen ⚜

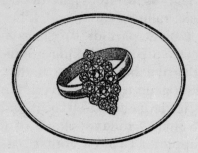

When school was over Friday, Christy asked David to go for a walk with her around Big Spoon Pond.

"Hoping the engagement ring washed up on shore?" David teased as they walked past the water's edge.

"I wish I *could* find it," Christy said. "Your mother would be so relieved. And it seems like the least I could do, after the way she helped me at school."

"I think she enjoyed feeling useful," David said.

"I still can't get over how smoothly teaching went this week, David!" Christy gave an embarrassed laugh. "If I hadn't let my stubborn pride keep me from asking for more help, I could have avoided a lot of pain."

"Actually, I've noticed the difference myself,"

David said. "When I teach the Bible and math classes, the children are more organized than I am these days. Yesterday afternoon we were working on multiplication, and John Spencer actually suggested I could use my time more efficiently if I divided the class into groups, according to ability."

"I have to admit, I'm glad to have Vella acting as chair monitor. I haven't sat on an egg all week!" Christy paused. She could hear the water lapping gently at the rocky shore. "Sometimes I think my blindness may be a blessing in disguise. I've learned a few things since losing my sight."

"Such as?" David reached for her hand, lacing his fingers through hers.

"Well, how wrong I can be, I suppose. I was so sure the only way to succeed at teaching was to do it all myself. Anything less would have been an admission of failure. But my pride and stubborness were wrong. I should have relied on God and my friends. It wasn't so hard to let others help me after all."

"Miss Alice says the doctor thinks it's time to remove your bandages," David said softly.

Christy nodded. "He's coming tomorrow morning. You know, I think I'm prepared, David. No matter what happens. If my sight never returns, I truly believe I can accept it and move on with my life."

David cleared his throat. "Christy, there's

something I wanted to mention to you. I heard about that walk in the woods you took with Dr. MacNeill, and I—" He paused. "Well, I just don't think that sort of thing is appropriate, now that you're engaged."

"Appropriate?" Christy echoed.

"It just doesn't look right. You understand."

"I'm not sure I do, actually." Christy hesitated. There was something else she wanted to say, but she simply didn't know how to begin.

"Miss Alice said something to me, David, after I accepted your proposal. She said it was important to be sure I was doing it for the right reasons."

"The right reasons," David repeated. He let go of her hand. She heard him scoop up a handful of stones. A moment later, she heard one skip lightly over the surface of the pond.

"I'm not sure . . . I'm not sure I made my decision for all the right reasons, David. I'm afraid maybe I was trying to prove something to myself. I wanted to prove that nothing had changed."

Another stone dropped into the water. "So," David said, his voice a whisper, "you're saying you don't love me?"

"I care for you deeply, David. I'm happy and content when I'm with you. I feel safe when I'm with you. But I'm not sure that's all there is to love."

"You're calling off the engagement," David said flatly.

Christy bit her lip. "For now. Just for now, until I can be sure about my reasons. I don't want you to marry me out of pity. And I don't want to marry you just to prove that my blindness hasn't changed me. The truth is, I *have* changed. But I'm beginning to accept that. Teaching this week, with the children pitching in, has helped me to see that I don't have to prove anything. The 'speriment, as Creed puts it, is over, I suppose."

"And you expect me to just accept that calmly? You betrayed me, Christy! You lied to me about how you felt!"

"I didn't lie, David. I just didn't know *what* I felt. I thought it was love. Maybe . . ." She took a shuddery breath. "Maybe it still can be. But I know I need more time. I was wrong about teaching, David. I don't want to be wrong about marriage, too. I hope you can find it in your heart to forgive me."

"I can forgive," David said angrily. "I'm just not sure I can forget."

— — —

"Now, I don't want you to expect too much," Doctor MacNeill cautioned Christy the following morning. "All the windows are covered, so it's quite dark in this living room. Assuming you can see anything, it's going to take awhile for your eyes to adjust."

"Assuming I can see anything," Christy

repeated with a smile. She could tell that Doctor MacNeill and the others were even more nervous than she was. She felt oddly calm. There was a great comfort in knowing that whatever happened, she was prepared to deal with it.

She heard the mission door open. "Am I too late?"

"David!" Christy cried. She was surprised he'd come. They hadn't spoken since yesterday. "I'm so glad you're here."

"Of course I'm here," he said softly.

"It's almost time for the great unveiling," Christy said.

"How she can joke at a time like this is beyond me," Mrs. Grantland muttered. "I'd be a nervous wreck."

"This will be like the other times I've changed your bandages," the doctor said to Christy. "Except that this time, I'll remove the dressing over your eyes, and I want you to very gradually open them."

"Wait a second, Doc," Ruby Mae said. Christy heard shuffling and the sound of furniture being moved.

"What *are* you doing, Ruby Mae?" Miss Alice asked.

"Movin' my chair up front, so as I can be the first thing Miz Christy sees."

Christy laughed. "Well, what are we waiting for, Doctor? I've dearly missed the sight of Ruby Mae's bright red hair."

Doctor MacNeill put a hand on her shoulder.

"I don't want you to get your hopes up, Christy. There's still some swelling. It may be too soon . . ."

"I understand. Really I do," Christy assured him.

Slowly the doctor began to unwrap her bandages. Christy could feel his fingers trembling.

At last the gauze that had been wrapped around her head was off, and all that remained were two large pieces of cotton dressing over her eyes.

"How do I look so far?" Christy asked.

"Pretty black and blue around your eyes," Ruby Mae reported.

"Kinda yellow and green, too," Creed added. "It's a mighty fine bruise, Teacher."

"All right, now, Christy," the doctor said. "I'm going to remove the cotton. The area around your eyes is still a bit swollen, so there may be some pain when you open them."

"Whatever happens," Christy said, "I want to thank you all for helping me through this."

"Here we go, then," the doctor said.

She felt the rough tips of his fingers as he gently pulled away the cotton. Her eyes felt strange, but she knew that was just because of the swelling.

Christy swallowed past the tight lump in her throat. Slowly she willed herself to raise her lids.

Nothing. There was nothing at all, nothing but darkness.

She took a deep breath. It was all right. She was going to be all right, no matter what.

It surprised her, how easily the feeling of peace and acceptance came to her.

"Well?" Ruby Mae asked in a hushed voice.

"I'm afraid I can't—"

Something changed. At the edges of the black mist, shadows formed and broke. The mist grew grayer, softer, like an early evening fog. "Wait," Christy whispered. "I see . . . I see light."

"Blink slowly a couple times," the doctor urged. "Don't try too hard to focus. Just let it happen."

Christy waited. Not a sound could be heard. Were they all holding their breath, just like she was?

A round, gray, shadowy form moved. Another came into her field of vision and left. Beyond the shadows was a square of some kind. It was a lighter color, almost a pale yellow.

A window? Was that a window?

Christy let her lids drop. Her whole head ached with the effort.

"Maybe it's too soon," Miss Alice suggested gently.

"No," Christy said. "I want to try again."

Again she opened her eyes. Shapes and colors blurred and danced. "Colors!" she whispered. "Blue! I see blue! And . . . red!"

She closed her eyes again and when she opened them, the tears began to fall.

It *was* red she'd seen. It was *very* red.

It was the tousled, wild, beautifully red hair of Miss Ruby Mae Morrison.

Christy turned her head slightly. She made out the slightly blurred image of a big man with a big smile.

"Neil," she whispered, "I can see!"

Without thinking, she threw her arms around him. He held her close, and in a voice only she could hear, whispered, "I'm so glad, Christy, so very glad."

She looked up and realized with a start that tears were streaming down the doctor's face. She'd never seen him cry before. She hadn't even though it was possible, somehow.

"Oh, Miz Christy," Ruby Mae exclaimed, "it's a miracle, is what it is. You must be feelin' as happy as a robin on the first day of spring!"

Christy pulled away from the doctor's arms, suddenly self-conscious. She *did* feel happy—gloriously happy—and so much more. What had made her throw her arms around Neil that way? Was it relief? Excitement? Or was it something more?

In an instant, everyone seemed to be hugging Christy at once. When she glanced over at the doctor, he was watching her with a tender smile as he wiped away his tears.

❧ Fifteen ❧

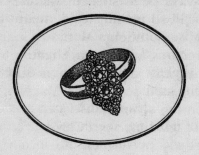

On Sunday afternoon after church, Miss Alice had a farewell picnic for Mrs. Grantland, who was leaving the next day. Everyone from Cutter Gap was there to enjoy good food and the beautiful spring afternoon. Each family brought something, however simple, to eat. Even Creed and Zach had contributed the three small fish they'd caught in the pond that morning before church.

Christy wandered the mission grounds as if she were walking through a spectacular dream. Doctor MacNeill had insisted that she wear a large sunbonnet to protect her eyes, but she could see all she needed to see. The grass had never been so green. The sky had never been so blue. Every sight, no matter how plain, was a gift.

But it was the faces of her students that

held the most magic. Had Creed's freckles always been so charming? Had Little Burl's eyes always been so deeply blue? How had she missed so much? Never again would she look at her students without marveling at their precious and unique beauty.

"Having my sight return is such a blessing," she said to Doctor MacNeill as they stood on the schoolhouse steps.

"I'm so glad for you, Christy."

"I feel so . . . so lucky."

"As it happens, so do I." The doctor gave her a knowing smile. "I heard you called off your engagement to David."

Christy gazed off at the mountain vista beyond the mission house. "I was doing it for the wrong reasons," she said at last. "But I couldn't admit it to myself." She shrugged. "Someone once told me I can be very stubborn."

"A wise man, indeed."

"I want to thank you, Neil."

"For what?"

"For being there when I needed you. And for being honest with me." Christy laughed. "I feel like I have so many thank-you's to say." She pointed across the yard, where Mrs. Grantland and David were talking. "Take Mrs. Grantland, for instance."

"David's mother? Are we talking about the same woman who disapproved of you from the start?"

"In spite of her feelings, though, she helped me. And I'm a better teacher because of her. Which reminds me . . . I have a presentation to make. Could you give me a hand?"

With the doctor's help, Christy gathered the children together and herded them over to Mrs. Grantland.

"My, what a procession!" Mrs. Grantland exclaimed. She gave David a questioning look. "What is all this about?"

"Ask Christy," David said. "I have no idea."

"Better yet," Christy said, "ask the children. Creed, why don't you explain?"

"We got somethin' for you, Miz Grantland, 'cause you're a-goin'," Creed announced.

"We made it last week," Ruby Mae added. "Instead of spelling lessons."

Mrs. Grantland looked at Christy. "You needn't have made them do this."

"I didn't. It was their idea completely."

"It's sorta to say thanks with the 'speriment and all. 'Cause you helped us talk Teacher into stayin'," Creed explained.

"Who's the gift monitor?" Christy asked.

"Me!" came a tiny voice. Vella stepped through the crowd. In her hand was a simple wooden box.

"Here, Miz Grantland," she said, holding out the box.

"Why! Why, it's a . . ." Mrs. Grantland examined the crude box, looking very confused.

"Well, it's a fine box, children. And I will most certainly think of a use for it. Perhaps . . . perhaps I could put pins and needles in it? Or maybe—"

"Naw, Miz Grantland, it ain't for puttin' into," said Zach. "It's already *got* stuff in it."

"Oh! My mistake." Mrs. Grantland opened the box. She stared at the bits of dried flowers and grasses inside. "Weeds!" she said, mustering a smile. "Well, I always say you can't have too many weeds—"

Christy could see how hard she was trying to be kind. "Smell them," she urged. "I think you'll understand."

Mrs. Grantland curled her lip a bit, but she bent toward the box and inhaled. Her eyes went wide.

"Roses!" she cried. "It smells just like roses!"

"It's dried wild rose petals and flowers and herbs and such," John Spencer explained.

"We knowed you'd like 'em on account of you always stinking like roses," Creed added helpfully.

Mrs. Grantland laughed, then breathed in the sweet-smelling box again. Christy was amazed to see a glimmer of tears in her eyes.

"In all my years of teaching, I've never had such a fine gift," Mrs. Grantland said. "Thank you, children."

"Thank you," Christy said. "I don't know what I would have done without your help.

To tell you the truth, to this day, I don't know why you helped me."

Mrs. Grantland shrugged. "I don't know. I suppose I liked feeling useful. With David and Ida all grown up, and my husband gone, it was nice to be needed for a while."

"You could always start teaching in Richmond again, Mother," David suggested.

"You could always start preaching in Richmond," she replied with a wink.

"I'm happy here," David told her gently.

"I can see that now," Mrs. Grantland said with a resigned sigh. "But a mother can still hope, can't she? Just think of all you're missing, David. The fine restaurants and fancy stores and—"

"And Delia Jane Manning," Christy added with a grin.

"She is a *fine* girl," Mrs. Grantland said wistfully. "She'd make some man a beautiful wife . . ."

"Well, it *does* seem I'm available once again," David said, avoiding Christy's eyes.

A frantic figure clad in a white apron rushed out of the front door of the mission house.

"Mother! Mother! David! Come quick!" Miss Ida screeched. She waved something silver in the air.

"That thar's one of our fishes!" Zach cried.

"Ida, dear!" Mrs. Grantland cried. "What's happened?"

"The ring! The ring!" Miss Ida cried frantically. She held up a tiny band with a cluster of diamonds on it. "I found it inside this fish!"

"Great-great-grandmother Grantland's ring, inside a fish!" Mrs. Grantland fanned her face, as if she might faint yet again. "We can only thank the good Lord she's not here to witness this!"

"Zach and I done caught the fish," Creed cried, "so we get the reward!"

"It looks like I'll have to come up with *two* copies of *Huckleberry Finn*," Christy laughed.

David took the ring from Miss Ida. It glimmered in the sun like a radiant promise. He gazed at Christy, shaking his head. For the first time, he began to smile.

"You don't suppose," he said, "that this is a good omen, do you?"

Christy smiled back. "Miracles do happen, David," she said. "At least, that's been my experience."

About the Author

Catherine Marshall

With *Christy*, Catherine Marshall LeSourd (1914–1983) created one of the world's most widely read and best-loved classics. Published in 1967, the book spent 39 weeks on the New York Times bestseller list. With an estimated 30 million Americans having read it, *Christy* is now approaching its 90th printing and has sold over eight million copies. Although a novel, *Christy* is in fact a thinly-veiled biography of Catherine's mother, Leonora Wood.

Catherine Marshall LeSourd also authored *A Man Called Peter*, which has sold over four million copies. It is an American bestseller, portraying the love between a dynamic man and his God, and the tender, romantic love between a man and the girl he married. *Julie* is a powerful, sweeping novel of love and adventure, courage and commitment, tragedy and triumph, in a Pennsylvania town during the Great Depression. Catherine also authored many other devotional books of encouragement.

#5—The Proposal

Christy should be thrilled when David Grantland, the handsome minister, proposes marriage, but her feelings of excitement are mixed with confusion and uncertainty. Several untimely interruptions delay her answer to David's proposal. Then a terrible riding accident and blindness threaten all of Christy's dreams for the future. (ISBN 0-8499-3918-6)

#6—Christy's Choice

When Christy is offered a chance to teach in her hometown, she faces a difficult decision. Will her train ride back to Cutter Gap be a journey home or a last farewell? In a moment of terror and danger, Christy must decide where her future lies. (ISBN 0-8499-3919-4)

Christy is now available on home videos through Broadman & Holman Publishers.